LOWTHAR'S BLADE TRILOGY · BOOK 3

THE **TRUE BLADE** OF **POWER**

LOWTHAR'S BLADE TRILOGY

❋ BOOK 3 ❋

THE
TRUE BLADE
OF POWER

R. L. LaFevers

DUTTON CHILDREN'S BOOKS

Copyright © 2005 by R. L. LaFevers

Library of Congress Cataloging-in-Publication Data

LaFevers, R. L. (Robin L.)
The true blade of power / by R.L. LaFevers.—1st ed.
p. cm.
Summary: In their ongoing attempt to destroy the power-hungry Lord Mordig, the young
human Kenric of Penrith and his Fey and goblin friends unite to create an invincible
sword to use in bringing peace to the kingdom of Lowthar.
ISBN 0-525-47431-5 (alk. paper)
[1. Swords—Fiction. 2. Goblins—Fiction. 3. Fairies—Fiction. 4. Fantasy—Fiction.]
I. Title.
PZ7.L1414Tr 2005   [Fic]—dc22   2004021584

Published in the United States by Dutton Children's Books,
a division of Penguin Young Readers Group
345 Hudson Street, New York, New York 10014
www.penguin.com/youngreaders

Map and title-page art by Hunter Brown

Printed in USA
First Edition
1 3 5 7 9 10 8 6 4 2

To my sons, Adam and Eric, for taking risks,
being brave, and for vanquishing the shadows
that have darkened their path

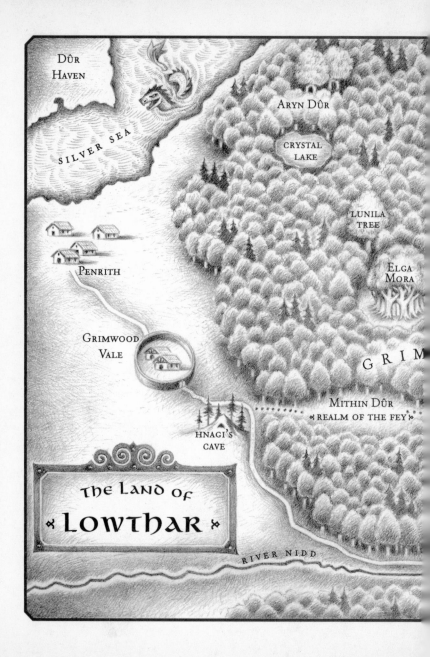

DÛR
HAVEN

SILVER SEA

ARYN DÛR

CRYSTAL
LAKE

LUNILA
TREE

ELGA
MORA

PENRITH

GRIM

GRIMWOOD
VALE

MITHIN DÛR
❧ REALM OF THE FEY ❧

HNAGI'S
CAVE

THE LAND OF
❧ LOWTHAR ❧

RIVER NIDD

HELGOR'S
TEETH

CARREG DHU
❖ GOBLIN REALM ❖

WARD
STONE

CRAGGYNESS

WOOD

TIRGA
MOR

OLD ROAD · · · ·

WINDEYVILLE

RIVER NIDD

HEMSBY
HEATH

N
W   E
S

LOWTHAR'S BLADE TRILOGY · BOOK 3

THE TRUE BLADE OF POWER

⁂ I ⁂

KENRIC'S SHOULDERS TWITCHED. His stiff new tunic itched, and his legs had fallen asleep. He was sure he had never sat through a dinner as long or boring as this one.

Next to him, Hnagi looked just as miserable. His head and shoulders drooped, and his feet dangled from his chair. He met Kenric's eyes and gave him a pleading look.

Kenric shrugged. There was nothing he could do. King Thorgil had insisted they attend the banquet being held in Princess Tamaril's honor.

He glanced to his right. Linwe looked as out of place as Hnagi. She looked like some forest creature who'd been captured and made a pet. The only one who was comfortable was the little hilfen, Dulcet. That was because she was curled up around Kenric's neck, fast asleep.

The adults around the table talked among themselves. Princess Tamaril sat at King Thorgil's right hand. The Fey smith Thulidor was on the king's left. Next to him was a wizened old stick of a man named Artemus. He was the royal historian and the king's closest adviser.

"How much longer do you think?" Linwe asked Kenric, keeping her voice low.

Kenric shrugged. "I have no idea. I've never been to one of these. You're a princess. Haven't you attended this sort of thing before?"

Linwe sniffed. "Not a human one."

Kenric was interrupted by a *ting*, *ting*, *ting*. He looked up to find the king tapping his spoon against his silver goblet.

Once everyone was quiet, he spoke. "Tonight we celebrate the return of our princess. With Mordig trapped in his stone prison, we were able to send out a search party to find her. Not only did they find her, but they also convinced the Fey to become our allies.

"I'd like to propose a toast to those who have served the kingdom so bravely. To Kenric of Penrith for his faithful service to his king. To Princess Linwe of the Fey, for risking so much to help him. And lastly to Hnagi, for agreeing to be their guide into the goblin realm."

"Hear, hear!" rang out around the table, then everyone drank to the toast. Kenric gave Linwe a look of embarrassment. Then he lifted his goblet to drink.

"No!" Linwe's hand shot out and stopped him. "You don't drink when you're the one being toasted," she whispered.

Kenric's cheeks flushed. He quickly set the goblet down, hoping no one else had noticed. He hated the stiff formality and pomp of this banquet.

After the toast, all eyes turned toward him. They were waiting for him to speak. The king caught his eye and nodded. Kenric gulped.

Linwe elbowed him. "Stand up!"

Kenric cleared his throat and bumbled to his feet. He stared at all the important people sitting at the table. Every word he'd ever known flew from his head.

He wiped his sweaty palms on his tunic and opened his mouth. Before he could speak, a loud rumbling noise rose up from the depths of the castle. The ground shook. Kenric reached out and grabbed the table to keep from falling. The harsh sound of rock creaking and grinding rang out through the hall. It was as if the very stones of the fortress were screaming.

There was one last deafening *crack*. King Thorgil

cried out, clutching his chest. Then he slumped back against his chair.

Princess Tamaril leaped from her chair and knelt beside her father. Artemus leaned forward to examine him. Confused voices erupted all around the room.

With a sickening jolt, Kenric remembered where he'd heard that sound before. "Come on," he said to Linwe and Hnagi. "I think I know what that was."

Linwe was on her feet in an instant, her dagger drawn. Hnagi shrunk back into his chair. "Hnagi stay here. Keep eye on king. Make sure he not—"

His words were cut off as Linwe reached out and hauled him to his feet. Kenric led them down the corridor to the Great Hall.

The Great Hall hadn't been used in weeks—not since Kenric had trapped Mordig in his stone prison. Taking a deep breath, Kenric reached out and opened the heavy doors.

It took his eyes a moment to adjust to the feeble torchlight in the room. It took a moment longer for his eyes to make sense of what he saw.

Mordig's stone prison was cracked wide open. Pieces of stone were thrown everywhere, as if the room had been blasted. The four guards posted on watch were all dead. They'd been struck by huge chunks of the rock as it flew apart.

Slowly, he turned to Linwe and Hnagi. "It's Mordig," he said. "He's escaped."

Linwe took a few cautious steps into the room, then stopped. "Are you telling me he was trapped in that stone?" she asked.

Kenric nodded. "I put him there."

Linwe whirled around to face Kenric. "You? How?"

"I used the bloodstone you gave me, along with a moonstone, and Hnagi's firestone. I also had a powerful blade that my father forged. Mordig had forced him to make it. He thought the blade would increase his power. But in the end, we were able to turn it against him."

Linwe folded her arms and frowned. "You aren't that strong."

Kenric smiled briefly at her disbelief. "True. But the stones are. I grabbed the sword away from the guard on my own. And I was so mad, I didn't stop to think. I just charged right for Mordig. The blade went through his armor, straight into the rock behind him. It sank in as easily as if it were cutting bread.

"Then the king whispered words for me to use. Words to call up the power of the three stones that I held. When I said those words, the rock rose up and swallowed Mordig. He's been trapped inside ever since."

Linwe stared at the wreckage in the room. "Then how did he get out?"

"I don't know," Kenric said.

❊ 2 ❊

A GUARD APPEARED in the hallway behind them. "The princess requests you come to the king's chambers," he announced.

"Of course," Kenric said.

The guard led them to the bedchamber. Princess Tamaril sat holding her father's hand. Next to her stood Artemus. Thulidor stood nearby, looking unsure of what to do with himself.

The princess waved them forward. As Kenric drew closer to the bed, his heart stumbled. King Thorgil was fading. His skin was pale. His hair was no longer white but almost transparent. With a shock, Kenric realized the king was becoming a wraith again.

"Has Mordig broken free?" the king asked, his voice thin and feeble.

"Yes," Kenric said. "The stone is ripped apart. Pieces of it crushed the four guards on duty."

The king opened his mouth to speak, then shook his head when no words came out.

Tamaril turned to Kenric. Even though her eyes were bright with unshed tears, she held her head high. When she spoke, her voice was strong and true. Kenric realized that she must have a core of steel, just like her father. He took hope from her strength, hope that not all would be lost now that King Thorgil had fallen ill.

"Do we know how Mordig was able to break free?" Kenric asked.

Artemus and Thulidor exchanged uneasy glances. "Not exactly, no," said Thulidor.

"But we can guess," Artemus added. "Mordig's power has grown greater than the king's. The king has no stones of power left to him. Mordig has at least two royal stones of power. He took King Thorgil's royal bloodstone when he defeated him the first time. This left the king weak and unprotected."

"We also know that Mordig has had King Valorin's royal moonstone for years," Thulidor said. "For all we know, he may have been able to get ahold of the royal firestone somehow. That's the only way he could have summoned the strength to break through that rock."

"Then why didn't he break through sooner?" Kenric asked. "Why did he wait so long?"

Artemus and Thulidor exchanged another look. "Once again," Thulidor said, "we can only guess. Perhaps he needed to rest after his defeat. Maybe he was waiting for help."

Artemus glanced over at the resting king. "Or maybe he just had to wait for the king to grow weak again. A body has only so much strength and resistance, no matter how strong the spirit." Artemus frowned, then shook his head. "Although it still makes little sense. Only one of royal blood should be able to command that much power through the stones. It should have been impossible for Mordig to break free."

"Does Mordig have royal blood?" Kenric asked. His words landed with a thud.

Tamaril's face grew pale, and her hand flew to her throat.

Artemus looked at the king, who shook his head weakly. "It can't be," he said. "It can't!"

"But, sire—"

"Impossible," said the king.

"But it *is* possible," Artemus said as gently as he could. "Your mother, Queen Iowith . . ."

"No!" the king shouted. He collapsed back against his pillows, weak with the effort. "My mother died years ago, when I was but a child."

"She disappeared, Your Majesty," Artemus gently reminded him. "But the body was never found. We don't know if she truly died."

"Are you saying Mordig is human?" Kenric said. "How can that be? He looks . . . different. Thicker, twisted somehow."

Hnagi shifted nervously. Kenric gave him a sharp look. "What do you know?"

The little goblin trembled. "Hnagi know Mordig have góblin blood."

Everyone turned to stare at Hnagi, who tried to hide behind Kenric's legs.

"Goblin blood!" Artemus and Thulidor said at the same time.

"Why didn't you say so before?" Kenric asked. "How do you know this?"

Linwe leaned down close to Hnagi's face. "What other secrets are you hiding from us?"

"Hnagi not keep secrets!" the little goblin said. "Know Mordig have góblin blood because he walk through fire to grab Hnagi. Only góblin walk through fire."

"He's right," Artemus said. "That's a power only goblins have."

Thulidor stroked his beard but said nothing. Finally, Kenric broke the silence. "Whatever or whoever Mordig is, we need to do something to stop him."

Tamaril stood up. She drew the curtains around her father's bed so they wouldn't disturb him. She motioned them to the far end of the room, where they could talk freely. "My father planned for Kenric and Hnagi to travel to the goblin realm, Carreg Dhu." The princess glanced at Linwe. "You may join them, if you wish."

Linwe nodded. "I will go."

"Princess!" Thulidor said in horror. "You cannot venture into the goblin realm! It is too uncertain."

Tamaril turned a cold eye to the Fey smith. "Are you saying that it is too difficult for a princess?" The steely tone of her voice suggested it would be unwise to think such a thing. Kenric knew in that moment she would go herself, if she were needed.

"No, no!" Thulidor shook his head. "Only that she is the heir to Mithin Dûr and shouldn't take such a risk. If something should happen to her . . ." The old smith's voice trailed off.

"It won't," Linwe said. But she laid her hand on Thulidor's arm to soften the words. "Besides, I must get my father's royal moonstone back. Without that, the Fey will always be vulnerable."

Hnagi shifted. "Not sure good idea. Góblin not like Fey. Could be nasty trouble."

Linwe pierced the little goblin with a look. "I'm going. That's the end of it."

Tamaril resumed her explanation. "My father wanted Kenric and Hnagi to obtain the goblin king's permission to forge a true blade of power on the goblin fires. Just as the Fey lore instructed. He also wanted them to speak with the goblin bards. Perhaps they have stories that tell of Mordig and where he came from. They may give us clues to defeating him."

"What you suggest makes sense, Princess," Kenric said slowly. "Except we don't have much time. I also wonder if we should follow Mordig and see where he goes. Then we can discover for ourselves where he comes from and where his stronghold is. Maybe then we can launch an assault—"

"There are not enough soldiers left to launch an assault on anything," the princess explained. "Our only hope is forging the blade and finding out how we can use it against Mordig."

Kenric shuffled his feet. "When we forge the blade this time," he asked, "will we need to bind it with blood?"

Princess Tamaril looked at him in surprise. "What?"

"When Mordig was trying to forge a blade of power, your father told me, 'Sweat is to make it, blood is to bind it.' I just wondered if we'd need to bind it in blood again."

Kenric flexed his hand. The scar still itched where he'd been cut when Mordig used his blood to bind the first blade.

Princess Tamaril turned to Artemus. "I've not heard of this. What does it mean?"

"I can answer that, if I may, Princess," said Thulidor. The Fey smith turned to Kenric. "For a blade to be truly great, the spirit of the smith must go into the making of it. All his knowledge and skill must be sweated into the blade. All the passion for his craft that runs in his veins must be poured into it. Without that, a blade is just another piece of worked metal."

"So that's what Mordig was doing wrong?" Kenric

asked. "He was using any blood when he should have been using the smith's blood?"

"Aye." Thulidor nodded. "But that was only part of it. When someone is forced to do something against their will, their heart and passion will not be in it."

"Do you know why the sword has to strike first in love? King Thorgil also said, 'Strike first in love, so evil can't find it.'" Kenric shuddered at the choice he'd had to make that day. He'd had to strike his father with the sword so Mordig couldn't use it for evil. It had been the hardest thing he'd ever done.

"The moment a sword draws its first blood is critical," Thulidor said. "That is the moment it will become an instrument of glory or evil. The first blood it draws will determine the spirit of the blade. Once a blade's been struck in love, whether love for a king or a country or a father, it is much harder to turn it to evil."

"Smiths will follow you to Carreg Dhu," Princess Tamaril said softly. "They will know what to do. Their wagons will carry the tools and materials you'll need to forge the sword. That way, as soon as you get permission, the smiths can begin. Thulidor is one. Your father is the other. He is on his way here, even as we speak. My father sent for him the moment you returned from

Grim Wood. They will be only two days behind you."

"Why didn't anyone tell me?" Kenric wanted to know.

Princess Tamaril shrugged. "Perhaps my father wanted to surprise you. Now come. We must map out your route to the goblin realm."

✣ 3 ✣

THEY STAYED UP well past midnight studying the king's maps. When Kenric finally reached his room, he threw himself facedown on his bed. He needed to get some sleep. It was foolish to begin such a journey exhausted. But even as his body lay still, his mind raced.

With luck, it would only be a two-day journey to the goblin realm. If they didn't get lost in the maze of mountains that surrounded it. And if the grymclaws or Mawr hounds or Sleäg didn't find them first.

Kenric also had a hard time seeing how the goblins were going to be any help. Hnagi was afraid of his own shadow half the time. Besides, Mordig had managed to sneak into Grim Wood. He'd found a way to get past the Fey patrol and weaken their king. Who was to say he hadn't done the same thing with the goblins?

THEY SET OUT the next morning before dawn. Kenric and Linwe hunched under the weight of their packs. Kenric stared into the gaping black hole that led deep into the belly of the fortress.

Princess Tamaril had come to bid them good-bye. Dulcet was perched on her shoulder, looking sad. "My father has placed much trust in you. You must convince the goblins to work with us. At the very least, we need their fires on which to forge our blade of power." The princess's voice echoed softly through the Great Hall.

"I will do my best, Princess," Kenric said. "And thank you for taking care of Dulcet. I'm afraid the goblins would see her as nothing but a juicy mouthful."

"It is my pleasure," she said, petting the little hilfen. "Remember the smiths will be two days behind you. I bid you a safe and productive journey."

Hnagi was the first one into the crater. He scampered over the side, then disappeared in the blackness.

"You go next," Linwe told Kenric. "Then I'll bring up the rear."

Kenric nodded, his heart lodged in his throat.

The stakes were so high this time. Everything was depending on them. It wasn't just his father or the princess.

The fate of man and Fey—the fate of the whole kingdom rested on their shoulders. If they failed, nothing would stand between them and Mordig's armies. Everything he knew, everyone he loved, would be in danger.

Kenric gritted his teeth. They would *not* fail. He took a deep breath, then slipped into the hole. He turned his body so that he faced the steep slope. His pack was heavy and kept him off balance. He fumbled his way down, using the fissures and outcroppings as footholds.

It seemed like forever before Kenric felt the firm ground beneath his feet. He stepped away from the rocky face he'd just climbed down. The tunnel was dark, the air warm and stale. There was very little light.

He could hear Linwe struggling up above. She grunted and her foot sent a small shower of rocks toward him. He turned his head aside to avoid the worst of it.

There was a tug on his pack that nearly had him tumbling backward. He turned to find Hnagi rubbing his hands.

"Thought Ken-ric never make it. Did Fey girl give up?"

"No," Linwe snapped through the darkness. "I'm still here." With a grunt and another small shower of scree, she reached the tunnel floor.

"Mordig's trail still fresh," Hnagi announced.

"How can you tell?" Kenric asked, peering against the dark.

"Goblins can see in the dark," Linwe explained as she adjusted her pack.

Hnagi nodded. "Hnagi see in dark. But not see Mordig trail. Hnagi smell that." The little goblin bent low to the ground and sniffed.

With his nose close to the tunnel floor, Hnagi began to lead the way.

After a few moments, Kenric's eyes adjusted to the inky blackness. He was able to put one foot in front of the other without stumbling. Then his foot hit something big and hard in the darkness. He lurched forward, the pack throwing him off balance. He reached out and groped at the wall, trying to keep from falling.

He steadied himself against the side of the tunnel. Closing his eyes, he took a deep breath to calm himself. When he opened them again, he gasped and jerked his hand away.

"What?" Linwe asked.

Kenric spread his palm against the wall again. Bright red drops shone in the blackness of the tunnel. When Kenric took his hand away, the red drops faded. "It's like the whole wall is made of bloodstones," he said.

"Here, let me see." Kenric heard Linwe fumbling with something, then a soft, white glow filled the tunnel. She came over to the wall and held her moonstone close. Hundreds of dull green bloodstones were stuck in the tunnel wall, as if they grew there.

Kenric touched one and the red drops flared to life. "I wondered where these came from."

"Well, now you know," Linwe said. "Now let's keep moving. I don't want to stay in here any longer than necessary."

Kenric opened the pouch in his pocket and drew out his own moonstone.

Hnagi was scrambling back to them. "Ai! Ai! Why have nasty stones out?"

"So we can see," Linwe said shortly.

"Now Hnagi can't see!"

"Well, we can't see without them," Linwe snapped.

"Can't you use your sense of smell?" Kenric asked the goblin.

With a sharp sigh of disgust, Hnagi nodded, then moved back to the front.

The tunnels grew damp and cool. The light from the moonstones showed openings in the tunnel walls. They must lead to more tunnels, Kenric realized. Passing those black, gaping holes made him uneasy. He tried not to think of what might lurk in there.

The longer they were in the tunnels, the more uneasy Kenric felt. He couldn't tell how much time had passed. Their plan had been to reach Craggyness by nightfall and spend the night there. But Kenric feared they were losing too much time here in the tunnels. He didn't want to be forced to spend the night out in the open. Now that Mordig was free, his servants were most likely growing in strength and numbers again.

He felt a flutter of fresh air drift past his face. Finally! They must be nearing the exit.

Just then, a stone rattled in the darkness behind him. His mind flew to the Mawr hounds that used to live deep within the tunnels of Tirga Mor. He strained, listening in the darkness.

"What?" Linwe asked, holding her moonstone out in front of her.

The pale glow didn't go far. Kenric stared, trying to see past the light. Was that shadow moving back there? Or did it just seem like it? "I'm not sure," he finally said. "I just thought I heard something."

"Do they patrol down here? Could you have heard guards?"

"Not that I know of. The only thing that lived down here was—"

A deep growl rumbled out of the shadow behind them. "Mawr hounds," Kenric finished. "Come on. Walk faster, but don't run."

As he picked up his pace, the growl grew louder. The hairs on the back of his neck prickled in alarm.

He glanced over his shoulder. There was a brief flicker of red. As Kenric adjusted his grip on his dagger, he nudged Linwe and motioned for her to move in front of him. As she did, a bone-chilling howl rang through the tunnel. Fear surged through Kenric, and he fought down the urge to bolt. He turned to Linwe. "Go!"

Linwe ran. Kenric heard the scrabble of clawed feet behind them. Giving in, he broke into a run, too. Hnagi turned around and saw them sprinting toward him. He started to run, but his goblin legs were short. He'd soon fall behind. Kenric and Linwe reached out, and each grabbed one of his arms, pulling him along between them.

Bright daylight spilled into the tunnel up ahead. Kenric's legs ached and his lungs burned, desperate for air. He dug deep inside and found one last burst of speed.

They reached the tunnel opening with the Mawr

hounds right on their heels. Kenric had only a second to realize it wasn't a cave mouth, but another crater with steep sides.

Hnagi jerked free of Kenric and Linwe. He scrambled up the crater like a small spider. Both hands free now, Kenric turned to face the hounds, dagger drawn.

The beasts slowed and bared their teeth. There were five of them. Thick strings of drool dripped from their open mouths. Kenric braced for their attack, but it didn't come. Puzzled, he looked around him. They were standing in a small circle of sunlight that poured in from the opening overhead. That was it! Mawr hounds had to keep to the shadows!

"Can you make it up that wall?" Kenric asked Linwe.

"Yes," she said. "Can you?"

"I'm not sure. Just get up there as quick as you can. Then I'll hand my pack up and follow. Hnagi," he called up to the little goblin. "See if you can find some rocks to throw. Distract the hounds while I try to climb up."

Linwe quickly made her way up the side of the crater.

Kenric backed up to the wall. He slipped his pack off his right shoulder, quickly pulling his dagger clear of the straps. Then he slipped it off his left shoulder.

The Mawr hounds inched closer. A black muzzle

poked into the sunlight, then jerked back with a whine. Kenric turned his body away from the hounds but kept his dagger pointed at them. Arm straining, he thrust his pack upward. Linwe snagged it on the first try.

The next move was the tricky part. He would have to turn his back on the hounds as he climbed. "Ready?" he called up.

"Ready," came Linwe's voice.

"Go!" Kenric shoved his dagger in his belt as a rain of stones began to pelt the hounds. They yelped in surprise. Kenric groped at the side of the crater looking for fingerholds.

He was halfway up before they realized he was escaping. He heard them leap forward. There was a snap of jaws near his leg, then a yelp as the sunlight drove the hounds back.

Suddenly there was a crackle and hiss. The crater floor erupted in blinding orange flame. The fire drove the Mawr hounds back even farther. Kenric scrambled to the top of the slope. Linwe and Hnagi grabbed his arms and hauled him up to safety.

❈ 4 ❈

"FIRE-DUST," KENRIC said between huge gulps of fresh air.

Hnagi nodded. "Tricksie góblin fire-dust better than rocks."

"It was the perfect distraction, Hnagi. Thank you." Kenric sat up. They had emerged from the tunnels of Tirga Mor into the bright noonday sun.

That had been close. Below them, the hounds yelped and snarled, trying to climb out of the crater. Luckily, the sun held them back.

"We can't rest too long," he said, pushing to his feet. "The hounds will be after us as soon as the sun goes down."

The road led to Craggyness, the only village between here and the goblin realm. Kenric took the lead. He spent the whole journey searching the shadows for signs of Mawr hounds.

They finally reached Craggyness two hours after nightfall. By then, Kenric's legs were cramping and his shoulders groaning under the weight of the pack. The streets were quiet. It looked like everyone was tucked in for the night.

"Keep an eye out for the largest building," Kenric told Linwe and Hnagi. "That will most likely be the tavern. We should be able to find food and shelter there." Hopefully. Kenric didn't say it out loud, but he was worried about the townspeople. How would they react to a goblin and a Fey? If they were as suspicious as the folks in Grimwood Vale, things could get ugly.

Kenric spotted the tavern in the middle of town. Bright lights spilled out from behind the shutters. With relief, he headed toward it. When he reached the door, he turned to Linwe and Hnagi. "It might be better if you wait out here. Let me see how friendly these people are first."

Kenric opened the door, it occurred to him that the men of Craggyness were a quiet bunch. There was no music or voices or clatter of crockery coming from within.

He pushed open the door and stepped inside.

There was no one there.

He turned and motioned the others inside. Plates of half-eaten food sat on the tables. Tankards lay on their sides in pools of ale. Linwe touched a loaf of bread. "It's still soft," she said, her voice quiet. "They haven't been gone long."

"But they certainly left in a hurry." A big, fat drop of fear rolled down Kenric's spine. "This isn't right," he muttered. Then he spoke louder. "We need to get out of here. Now." He turned and shoved Linwe and Hnagi back toward the door. They stumbled outside straight into a pack of snapping, slavering Mawr hounds. They leaped back into the tavern and slammed the door. There was a shuddering *thud* as the hounds hurled themselves against it. Frustrated, the hounds began their blood-curdling howls. Every hair on Kenric's head stood up in alarm.

"Now what?" asked Linwe.

Kenric glanced frantically around the room. He heard a creak on the floorboards above. His eyes went to a dark stairway leading to the upper floors.

There was another creak. "A trap!" Kenric spun around, still searching for an escape route or a hiding place. Anything!

He spied a ladder behind the bar. It led up to a loft, likely a storage area where the innkeeper kept his supplies. "Come on!" He grabbed Hnagi's arm and rushed to the ladder. He shoved Hnagi up onto the rungs. The goblin struggled as he found his footing, then scrambled up.

There was another creak behind Kenric. He grabbed Linwe and practically lifted her onto the ladder. "No!" she argued. "I'll bring up the rear!"

"Get up there. Now!" Kenric said, giving her a mighty boost.

A tall figure stepped off the stairs into the room. He was cloaked all in black. A Sleäg!

"His Lordship thought you would be foolish enough to follow," the Sleäg said.

A second Sleäg appeared at the top of the steps leading up from the cellar. He turned to watch Hnagi and Linwe hurry up the ladder. He threw his head back and laughed, exposing his skeletal face. "What? You think Sleäg can't climb?" He took a step forward.

Linwe had almost reached the top rung. Kenric grabbed hold and stepped on. The rickety ladder wobbled under his weight. He looked over his shoulder. The Sleäg were moving toward him slowly, as if they were enjoying the chase.

Deciding he'd risk the rickety ladder, Kenric scrambled up as fast as he could. As he drew near the top, Linwe grabbed his pack and hauled him up into the loft.

Quickly, he reached around to pull in the ladder.

But one of the Sleäg already had a foot on the bottom rung. Kenric kicked at the ladder and sent it toppling over onto the tavern floor below.

"They'll just put it back," Linwe said.

"I know, but it will buy us a few extra minutes," he said as he rolled to his feet. "There's got to be a way out of here." He crossed over to where the sloping roof reached the attic floor. He tried to shove aside the thatching. "Look! Over there. A barn. We'll have to jump."

Hnagi shook his head. "No. No jump. Too far. Hnagi go splat."

"No, you won't. Watch." Kenric motioned Hnagi closer. As the goblin drew near, Kenric grabbed him. "Sorry, Hnagi," he muttered. Then he picked him up and heaved him across the space. Hnagi squealed as he flew, then hit the thatched roof of the barn with an *oomph*. He tumbled straight through the straw into the barn. Kenric pulled off his pack and threw it after Hnagi, making sure it landed away from him.

Kenric turned to Linwe. She glared at him. "I can do it myself."

"I never doubted," Kenric said. He pulled back so Linwe could get out on the ledge next to him. He held her pack as she slipped out of it.

He heard a *thunk* as the ladder was put back in place. "Hurry!"

She took a deep breath and leaped across the open space, never looking down. Kenric held his breath until she landed in the thatch and disappeared beneath it. He flung her pack after her, then got ready for his own jump.

He stood poised on the edge of the tavern roof. He heard the creak of a ladder rung as weight was put upon it. Suddenly the distance looked much farther than it had before. He wished he could take a running start. He also wished he were smaller and lighter of foot, like Hnagi or Linwe.

There was another creak as the first Sleäg stepped into the loft.

Refusing to think about it another second, Kenric took a deep breath and leaped.

⊰ 5 ⊱

KENRIC SAILED THROUGH the air, then crashed into the roof of the barn. The thatching poked and scratched at him as he fell through. He landed with a bone-racking thud that knocked the breath clean out of him.

He opened his eyes to find Linwe and Hnagi peering down at him. Hnagi reached out and pinched him.

"Ouch! What was that for?"

"To see if Ken-ric all right. And for tossing Hnagi."

Kenric eased into a sitting position, grateful to find that no bones were broken. He saw they had all landed on a loft that took up half the barn. If not for the loft, they would have fallen all the way to the bottom.

"We need to get out of here before they figure out where we've gone," Linwe said.

Kenric nodded. "Let's go." He tossed their packs down to the barn floor while Linwe and Hnagi hurried down the ladder.

Kenric was right behind them. They shrugged into their packs. Kenric's shoulders groaned in protest. At the door, he paused and peeked out.

Nothing.

He could tell by the snarling that the hounds were still guarding the tavern door. The Sleäg hadn't followed them yet, either. Maybe they hadn't been able to tell where he and Linwe and Hnagi had gone. The roof thatching of the barn had hidden them well.

Clinging to the shadows against the wall, Kenric crept out into the night. When he was certain the coast was clear, he motioned the others to follow. As Linwe stepped out of the barn, he saw the glint of her drawn dagger. Realizing that was a good idea, Kenric drew his own.

Keeping the barn between themselves and the Sleäg, they struck out. Whenever possible, they hid in the shadows of the abandoned buildings. Kenric couldn't help but wonder what had happened to the people of Craggyness. He hoped they'd managed to flee to safety.

When they reached the edge of town, there were still no sounds of pursuit. Kenric should have been glad, but he couldn't help fearing another trap. Still, they had no choice but to keep going.

The night air was still and cold. He looked over at Linwe, whose face was grim. Hnagi didn't look too happy, either. He scuttled along in a zigzag pattern, always trying to move from one sheltered spot to the next.

Kenric's muscles ached. He had been desperate for a rest. His pack felt as if it weighed as much as two cows. His eyes were gritty with lack of sleep. Worse yet, his nerves were strung tight. Every whisper in the wind sounded like a Sleäg. Every rustle of leaves made him jump, certain a Mawr hound was about to burst from the bushes.

As the night wore on, their steps became slower and slower. Soon they were almost asleep on their feet. Kenric shook himself. They had to find someplace to get some rest. They couldn't march straight through. There was no telling what waited for them in the goblin realm.

The rows of fields had given way to scrubby meadow littered with rocks. Huge rocks, Kenric realized as the moon glinted off a nearby standing stone. It was nearly as tall as he was.

"Getting closer to góblin realm." Hnagi's voice at his elbow made Kenric jump.

He glanced down at the goblin. "We need to find a place to sleep for a few hours. Keep your eyes open for some kind of shelter."

"Cave?" Hnagi asked hopefully.

"No!" Linwe answered.

Kenric shook his head. "She's right. We could be trapped too easily in a cave. We need someplace where we can see all around us but have something at our backs. Like sleeping in a tall tree, that kind of thing."

Hnagi shuddered. "No trees here. Only rocks."

True. And the farther they walked, the bigger the rocks grew. They were now three times as tall as a man, and many of them were nearly as wide as a house.

"How about there?" Linwe said, pointing to a large rocky hilltop. It was tall and flat and would allow them to see any Sleäg or hounds approaching.

"Perfect," Kenric said. He picked up his pace, eager for even a short rest.

THE NEXT THING Kenric knew, early daylight was nudging his eyes open. He rolled over and stretched his aching muscles. When he opened his eyes fully, the sky was tinted gold and orange as the sun flared to life. It almost looked as if the circle of mountains were on fire.

With a sigh, he got up and woke the others. They ate a rushed breakfast of bread and cheese, then made their way off the hilltop.

They trudged their way through the morning in silence. They needed to save all their strength for their travels.

It seemed to Kenric that no matter how much they walked, the mountains never got any closer. Then, shortly before sunset, they suddenly loomed just ahead, like a ring of giant teeth. They all stopped and stared, dismayed at the sheer size and height of the mountains.

"Do we have to climb those?" Linwe asked.

Hnagi shook his head. "No. Cut through mountains. Use passes."

"Then let's get going," Kenric had hoped to reach Carreg Dhu before nightfall. If they couldn't do that, they would need to look for shelter again. He'd had a sense of being followed all day. The mountains might not offer much protection against their enemies.

Kenric saw something move up ahead. He blinked, trying to clear his eyes.

"Hnagi," Kenric said, keeping his voice low. "Are the boulders in Carreg Dhu able to move around on their own?"

Hnagi snorted with laughter. "Stupid hu-man! Boulders not walk!"

"Well, then what are those?" Kenric pointed up ahead. Two boulders were heading their way.

✳ 6 ✳

Hnagi stopped walking and his ears drooped. He inched toward Kenric. "Not boulders. Góblin," he whispered.

Kenric gaped. He looked at the massive goblins, then back at Hnagi. "B-but they don't look anything like you!"

Hnagi shrugged. "Different caste."

"Caste?" Linwe repeated. "You mean like a class system?"

Hnagi nodded, clearly miserable. "These Urgol. Hnagi only finnboggi."

Kenric watched in horrified fascination as the Urgol goblins drew closer. They were half again as tall as Kenric's father, and three times wider through the shoulders and chest. Their arms were thicker than Kenric and hung to their knees. They carried savage-looking axes.

The goblins stopped in front of Kenric, Linwe, and Hnagi. One of them hefted his ax high into the air. He brought it crashing down onto the ground, leaving a deep gash in the earth.

"Who dares enter Carreg Dhu?"

Kenric looked over at Hnagi shivering beside him. He gave the goblin a nudge forward.

The giant goblin's tiny eyes widened in surprise. "A finnboggi?" He turned and spit into the rocks.

"Have enough puny finnboggi in Carreg Dhu," the second goblin said, his voice rumbling like a shower of stones down a hill. "Don't need more."

Kenric waited for Hnagi to say something. Anything!

Finally, with one last glance at Kenric, Hnagi stepped forward. "Even if finnboggi bring prisoners for King Orlegg?"

Prisoners! Kenric stared at Hnagi. The small goblin wouldn't meet his eyes.

The Urgol's eyes widened in surprise, then they burst out laughing. One of them reached out and gave Hnagi a friendly thump on the back that nearly knocked him down. "Ha! Good job, little finnboggi! King Orlegg be pleased."

The second Urgol frowned. "Why prisoners not tied up?"

"Prisoners promise not run away."

"Ha! Stupid finnboggi! Prisoners always lie. Here, Hlogg tie up for you." Hlogg stepped forward and pulled a thick leather rope from his belt. As the goblin stepped closer, Kenric jerked his head back and his eyes watered. The Urgol reeked of rotten meat and sulfur.

Hnagi hurried forward. "Hnagi's prisoners! Hnagi tie!"

Hlogg studied the little goblin a moment before tossing the coil of leather rope at him. The heavy coil knocked Hnagi flat on his backside.

As Hnagi struggled to his feet, Linwe leaned over to Kenric. "What's he up to?"

"I have no idea."

"Should we trust him?"

Kenric nodded firmly. "Maybe this is the fastest way to get to the king. Besides, if we're with these two, I don't think the Sleäg or Mawr hounds will dare attack us tonight."

Linwe didn't say anything, but Kenric could see she liked that idea.

When Hnagi came over to tie his hands, Kenric whispered, "I sure hope you know what you're doing."

Hnagi glanced over his shoulder at the Urgol, who

were watching them. "Quiet, prisoner!" the little goblin yelled.

Kenric blinked in surprise.

Hnagi moved over to Linwe and began tying her up. The Fey girl said nothing, but she scowled at Hnagi the entire time.

When both prisoners were secure, Hlogg stepped forward. "Come. Urgol take finnboggi to king. In case finnboggi need help."

Kenric leaned over to Linwe one last time. "At least they didn't blindfold us like you did," he said.

She threw him a withering look, which cheered him up a bit.

The sun had completely set by now, but the sky still had an eerie reddish glow to it. They wove their way between towers of rock and thick boulders. They passed a bubbling, black pool that reeked of sulfur. Now and then, a geyser of liquid fire would shoot straight up into the sky in a shower of sparks. Luckily, Kenric's hands were tied in front so he was able to slap at the sparks to keep from catching fire.

As Kenric passed one of the bubbling red-and-black pools, he heard a hiss. He jerked his head up and saw a long shape slithering out of the bubbling mess.

It was long, as long as Kenric was tall, and as thick as his leg. It glowed red as it crept from the pool to the rocks. At first Kenric thought it was a serpent, but it was unlike any he had seen before. A row of jagged spikes ran down its back. The spiked tail twitched back and forth. Long pointed barbs flared out around its head, and it had a blunt snout. A skinny red tongue flicked toward Kenric. The creature coiled its body, and Kenric realized it was about to strike.

There was a blur of motion, then the sound of rock being split in two. Kenric blinked and saw one of the Urgol holding a bloody ax. The serpent creature lay in two pieces, both of them wriggling and steaming on the splintered rock.

"Nasty wyrm!" the Urgol muttered. "Kill finnboggi prisoner before Great One ever see."

Kenric forced his knees to quit knocking and stumbled after the others. Linwe's face was pale and drawn as she stepped over the writhing mess.

Kenric quickly realized he could never find his way out of these mountains on his own. But at least there was a good chance the Sleäg and Mawr hounds wouldn't be able to follow them.

Just when Kenric was sure he couldn't go on, they

reached an especially jagged area of rocks with sharp spires that thrust into the sky. As they drew closer, Kenric saw a giant cavern with a gaping mouth that led deep into the mountains. More goblin guards were posted on either side. Urgol, by the looks of them. Long, sharp stone daggers hung at their hip. Battle-axes were strapped across their backs.

As their small group approached, the two guards stepped forward, crossing their spears.

Hlogg spoke. "Hlogg and Fangr from southern watch. Bring prisoners to Great One."

The guards studied the small group. One of them used the butt of his spear to prod Hnagi. The little goblin lurched backward. "Finnboggi not big enough to be prisoner."

Fangr shoved the guard back a few steps. "Finnboggi under Hlogg and Fangr protection. These prisoners!" He thrust his hand toward Kenric and Linwe. "Not finnboggi."

The guard grunted and bared his teeth at Fangr. Then he moved aside to let them pass. Kenric let out a breath he hadn't realized he'd been holding.

He followed the Urgol into the cavern, stunned at how enormous it was. He tipped his head up.

Long spikes of rock hung down from the mountaintop, like spears shoved toward the earth. Towers and spires of rock thrust upward from the cavern floor. Openings, large and small, led from the main cavern in all directions.

The air was hot and suffocating. It reeked of swamp mud. Kenric tried breathing through his mouth, but that was worse. He could taste it on the back of his tongue.

As their guards led them through the cavern, all the goblins stopped. Hundreds of green, yellow, and orange eyes stared at them. Some of the goblins pointed and jeered.

They were all so different, Kenric thought. Some of the goblins were huge and thick and mud-colored, like Fangr and Hlogg. The yellowish ones seemed to be around the same size as men, but heavier, with shorter legs. The smallest goblins, the ones who looked like Hnagi, were a greenish brown color. They scuttled back and forth carrying trays or buckets, or pushing small carts.

Hnagi ignored the jeers and walked with his head held high. A low drumbeat started up, silencing the crowd of goblins. It seemed to come from deep within the mountain. With each beat, Kenric's nerves grew tighter. Leaning down, he asked, "What is that, Hnagi?"

"Góblin drums. Let everyone know prisoners arrive."

Urgol formed a line in front of the entrance to the next

cavern. They nodded at Fangr and Hlogg and let them pass without questions. This new cavern was smaller than the main one, but more impressive.

The black rock spires were more delicate here. Fancier. Several small pools of fire pitted the cavern floor. Kenric jumped as a geyser of liquid fire spouted from the pool closest to him. After a stunning shower of red and orange sparks, the geyser died back down.

At the far end of the room sat an enormous goblin. He was half again as big as Fangr and Hlogg. His skin was mud colored, his small eyes the color of copper. An enormous firestone hung from his neck, winking brilliant orange light. One of the hideous wyrm creatures lay coiled at his feet. This one was black. As they approached, it opened its bright green eyes and hissed.

Hlogg and Fangr halted and pushed Hnagi forward to stand in front of the goblin king.

Kenric could see Hnagi's knees knocking. The poor goblin's ears were down and trembling like leaves in a breeze. Hnagi threw himself facedown on the floor. His hands stretched out to the king. "Please, O Great One. Poor Hnagi bring honored prisoners in exchange for Great One's pardon!"

❧ 7 ❧

King Orlegg squinted at Hnagi. "Pardon Hnagi? Orlegg never pardon weak, rotten coward! You cast out of góblin realm! Told never come back. Hnagi disobey, Hnagi die. Guards!"

Kenric's mind scrambled. What could Hnagi have done to earn the goblin king's wrath?

Hnagi flinched and groveled harder. "Wait! Bring prisoners as gift. Message from hu-man king. O Great One must hear. Poor Hnagi ask for private meeting. Have much for your ears only."

The goblin king studied the prisoners. His sly eyes narrowed. He turned to Hnagi. "Finnboggi bring me Fey and hu-man. For this, will see him alone. Then kill him." He looked up at his guards. "Out!" He motioned with his hand.

Grumbling, Fangr and Hlogg made their way to the cavern door. Orlegg turned back to Hnagi. "Now, finnboggi. Speak. Secrets better be good!"

Hnagi pushed himself to his knees and hobbled closer to the king's throne. He turned and motioned for Kenric and Linwe to come forward. "O Great One. Hnagi bring important words from hu-man and Fey kingdoms."

Orlegg glanced at Kenric and Linwe. "From prisoners?"

Hnagi shook his head so hard his ears flapped. "Not prisoners. Most honored ambassadors. Hu-man king trust them to Hnagi's care. Hnagi ask Great One permission to untie."

Orlegg scowled. "Why Orlegg pardon weak, cowardly finnboggi? Not even bring prisoners!" The goblin king shook his head in disgust. "Go ahead. Untie."

When Hnagi had cut his bonds, Kenric cleared his throat and stepped forward. "Please, O Great One," he said. "Honorable Hnagi has brought something better than two small prisoners. He brings a chance to reforge the alliances of old. King Thorgil and Princess Tamaril of Tirga Mor request you join with them to battle the threat of Mordig. Princess Linwe of the Fey has already agreed to join—"

"Fey? Hu-man king talk to Fey first?"

"Er . . ." Kenric glanced frantically at Linwe. "It was an accident, really. I had to go to the Fey realm to search for the Princess Tamaril. She'd been hiding there ever since Mordig first came to power. While I was there, the Fey learned what was happening and agreed to join us."

Orlegg stopped scowling and gave a little nod.

Kenric continued. "The Fey lore claims there is only one way to defeat Mordig. We need a true blade of power. The old lore says this can only be made by goblin, man, and Fey working together. A Fey smith and a human smith need to forge the sword over goblin fire. King Thorgil asks your permission to do this. We'd also like the chance to talk to your historian. We need to learn all we can about Mordig if we are to defeat him."

"Why think góblins know about him?" the goblin king asked.

"We just hoped that there might be some information in your lore."

"Hmm. Góblin don't do scratchings on paper. Not have historian. Use bard. But no bard right now. Grow old. Not able to tell stories anymore."

Kenric's spirits sank.

"These serious matters," Orlegg said. "Why king trust them to cowardly finnboggi?"

Why did the king hate Hnagi so much? Kenric needed to try to change Orlegg's opinion of the little goblin. And fast. "Hnagi has proved himself brave many times. The human king trusts him. Hnagi went with me into Grim Wood—"

"The realm of the Fey?" Orlegg was clearly surprised.

"Yes. He, er, guarded my back and stood up to the entire race of Fey. He helped win their support for King Thorgil. He even sacrificed his blood when we stood against Mordig."

"This lazy cowardly finnboggi did?"

"Yes!" Which was true. Sort of. "He braved grymclaws and Mawr hounds. He even lent me his firestone so I could call upon the power of the stones to defeat Mordig!" Kenric added.

Orlegg's eyes widened, and he began fiddling with the enormous wart on his chin. "Ken-ric can call on power of stones?"

Kenric nodded.

Orlegg's eyes narrowed and a sly, cunning look crossed his face. Kenric didn't like it one bit. But at least the king wasn't talking about sending Hnagi to his death anymore.

"Tell me more of this blade."

"A true blade of power must be forged by all three races working together. The strength of the blade is linked to the alliance of the three races."

The goblin king's eyes grew bright. "Hmm," he grunted, letting go of his wart. "Orlegg grant permission to forge blade on góblin fire."

Relief surged through Kenric, and he stepped forward. The wyrm hissed at him, and he hastily stepped back. "Thank you, Great One. Does this mean you have decided to join the human and Fey alliance?"

"Alliance not simple thing. Take much thought. Must weigh choices. If ally with hu-man and Fey, Mordig make bad enemy. Do hu-man and Fey have strength to help góblins against him? How Orlegg know Fey and hu-man strong enough? What if Orlegg fight with Fey and man, but Mordig still win? What then? Góblin closest to Mordig. Góblin get most of his wrath. Orlegg must weigh all this."

"Together we can beat him. King Thorgil is certain," Kenric said. "Especially if we have a true blade of power. Even Mordig shouldn't be able to stand against that."

Orlegg shifted his gaze away from Kenric. "Big decision," the goblin king said. "Orlegg think more. Then decide."

"If we don't all work together—"

Orlegg slammed his meaty fist down on the arm of his throne. The wyrm hissed a small stream of fire. "Enough!" he bellowed. "Orlegg must think."

Kenric's mouth snapped shut, and he took another step back.

Orlegg barked out an order and two finnboggi came running. They did a double take when they saw Hnagi.

"Take guests to quarters," Orlegg commanded.

With a worried glance at Hnagi, one of them asked, "What about cowardly finnboggi, O Great One? Dungeon for Hnagi?"

Orlegg considered for a moment. "No. Finnboggi stay with guests. Be guide. For now."

"Thank you, Great One," Hnagi said.

Keeping a close eye on the wyrm, Kenric asked, "When may we speak with your smith? The human and Fey smiths will be here in two days. I'd like to give him some warning."

Orlegg waved his hand. "Hnagi show you to smith in morning."

Hnagi stepped forward, ears back. "O Great One.

Poor Hnagi happy to show hu-man and Fey goblin realm. But—" He stopped and shuffled his feet, clearly uneasy. "Will Urgol and gurfig let Hnagi?"

Orlegg frowned. "Here," he said, reaching up to his throat. For one brief moment Kenric thought he was going to give them the giant firestone that hung around his neck. Instead he plucked a jagged piece of black metal from his cloak. He tossed it to Hnagi. "Show this. Say Orlegg send you."

Standing tall, Hnagi caught the brooch and affixed it to his belt. Then he bent low to the ground in a deep bow. "Thank you, O Great One."

With very surprised looks, the two little finnboggi motioned for the trio to follow them. The one in front began muttering. "Why cowardly finnboggi return? Bring shame on all finnboggi!"

"Hush, Glumgi!" the other little goblin said. "Hnagi bring great honor on finnboggi with prisoners. Hnagi carry O Great One's seal. No finnboggi ever do that before! Great honor!"

The two servants continued arguing until they reached a medium-size cavern. They showed Kenric, Hnagi, and Linwe inside, then bowed low and left.

Kenric looked uneasily at his new surroundings. The

room was nothing but slabs of rock and lumps of stone. A large, bubbling fire pit sat in the middle of the room. Liquid fire and rock gurgled and hissed. "Why are the finnboggi so looked down upon?" Kenric asked as he slipped off his pack.

"Not big and strong. Can't fight. Small. Weak. Only good for grunt work."

"Then it's the Urgol who're in charge?"

Hnagi nodded. "Urgol rule. In charge. Warriors. Kings. Strong."

"What about the medium-size ones I saw out in the hallway? Who are they?"

"Gurfig. Bigger than finnboggi. Smaller than Urgol. Not warriors. Not kings." Hnagi shrugged. "Not servants. Make weapons. Work leather. Build things."

"What else have you not told us?" Linwe asked, her voice laced with anger. "Why does your king hate you so much?"

"Not Hnagi's fault! Swear it!"

Kenric turned to the little goblin. "Tell us what happened, Hnagi. I need to know how it will affect our mission."

Hnagi stared at the cave floor and shuffled his feet.

"Long time ago, Hnagi part of western patrol. Prince Durrig, O Great One's son, lead patrol. Check borders. Search caves for black metal. Always lots of finnboggi on patrols. Patrols need hard workers," he said with pride.

"Set up camp. Begin mining. Find good ore." Hnagi looked into the fire pit as he remembered. "Mine for two days when Mordig come. Not Mordig," Hnagi corrected. "Mordig servants. Sleäg, nasty dog, grymclaws." Hnagi shuddered. "Whips and chains. Fighting and shouting. Get prince first. Wrap in chains of Fey silver. Make prince weak. Then scoop up finnboggi. But Hnagi hide. Sniffing nasty dog almost find. But Sleäg call him back."

Linwe's eyes narrowed as she studied Hnagi. "He probably wanted one person to escape. Then they could carry the tale back to your king."

The little goblin nodded. "Hnagi did. Orlegg crazy mad. Shout. Yell. Throw Hnagi in dungeon. Say Hnagi's fault. Finally, after two years, let Hnagi go. Say never come back."

"And yet you did," Kenric said quietly. "You agreed to be our guide. Even though you knew you'd be in danger." How brave Hnagi had been, and none of them had known it.

Hnagi's face scrunched up in a fierce scowl, and he clenched his fists. "Only way stop Mordig. Make things safe again. Hnagi want to come home."

Linwe frowned, puzzled. "But you're a finnboggi, right?"

Hnagi nodded.

"Then they know you're weak and small and not good for fighting. Why did King Orlegg expect you to save Prince Durrig? You don't have the strength. None of the finnboggi do."

Hnagi hung his head. "No. But Hnagi must die trying. Hnagi not put his life before prince's." The little goblin shook his head.

"Well, that's ridiculous!" Linwe said.

Just then, the two finnboggi reappeared carrying trays. To Kenric and Linwe's horror, and Hnagi's delight, they held platters of raw meat. With furtive glances at Hnagi, the two finnboggi set the trays down. Hnagi hurried over to the tray. The littlest finnboggi reached out and touched him. Hnagi jumped, slapping the hand away.

The little finnboggi threw himself facedown on the ground. "Sorry, Most Honored finnboggi," he said. "Nuugi just want to touch your greatness. No finnboggi ever bring prisoners before."

Hnagi looked at Kenric, who shrugged. Slowly, Hnagi held out his arm.

Nuugi rose to his feet. Then he reached out and touched Hnagi's arm with one finger. He nodded his thanks, then left the room. The second finnboggi, Glumgi, just stared.

"I think you're becoming famous," Linwe teased. "A little goblin like you capturing two big bad prisoners."

Hnagi grinned, and the tips of his ears darkened. Then he turned to his meal, tearing into the raw meat with his daggerlike teeth.

❈ 8 ❈

THEY WERE AWAKENED the next morning by the sounds of little feet. Three finnboggi came in carrying breakfast trays and water. They stared at Hnagi as if he were some sort of hero. With a nervous glance at Kenric, one of them spoke.

"Brave finnboggi," the little servant said. He nodded, then clasped his fist to his heart.

Hnagi stared at him. Finally he nodded and brought his own fist up to his heart. Pleased, the servant scampered back to the others. They whispered their way to the door.

Linwe stared at the tray the finnboggi had left. "Raw meat again."

"That what góblin eat," Hnagi explained, digging in.

Linwe shook her head in disgust and pulled some bread and cheese out of her pack. Kenric wasn't about to eat raw meat, but he was sick of the hard, stale bread he carried. Instead he pierced his slab of meat with his dagger. Then he carried it over to the bubbling geyser of liquid fire and held it out to roast.

"We should try to see Orlegg first thing this morning," Kenric said. "I want to see if he's decided whether or not to join the alliance."

Hnagi shook his head. "No. Will send for when has decision. Best not to pester."

Kenric thought about it for a moment. "You're probably right. In that case, I say we start at the forge this morning."

THEIR SMALL GROUP was stopped just outside the forge by an Urgol guard. "Where finnboggi think he going?"

Hnagi stood tall, his head up and his shoulders thrown back. He proudly flashed the brooch Orlegg had given him. "On business for Great One. Take Great One's guests to smith."

The Urgol's eyes blinked at the shiny black brooch. Grumbling, he let them pass.

They stepped into a large cavern. It was hotter than anyplace Kenric had ever been in his life. Within seconds, sweat began to trickle down his neck.

Large craters pitted the rocky floor. Liquid fire and

rock bubbled and boiled inside them. The cavern echoed with a continuous tapping and hammering. Groups of finnboggi were hard at work, chipping away at the black metallic stone the goblins used for their blades.

A large group of gurfig goblins clustered around the bubbling fire pits. Every few seconds, a geyser of flame and molten lava burst into the air. Each time, one of the gurfig would reach out and snatch something from the jet of fire. The gurfig would scuttle off a few feet to squat on the floor and hammer at the small, charred piece of rock. Kenric stepped closer to see better. With a crunch, all the black fell away. A glittering orange-and-blue lump lay on the floor. A firestone, Kenric realized.

Slowly, the goblins realized there were strangers in their midst. One by one they stopped what they were doing and stared. Finally one stepped forward. Kenric was fairly certain he was a gurfig. He was medium size, but his arms and shoulders were massive, almost as large as those of an Urgol. His face was as wrinkled and brown as an old walnut. "Why finnboggi bring hu-man and Fey to Kraag's forge?" The goblin turned and spit into one of the craters. The fire flared briefly.

Trying to keep his knees from knocking, Hnagi showed Kraag his brooch from the king. "O Great One send Hnagi. Show hu-man and Fey góblin forge."

The smith snorted in disbelief.

"Our land is being threatened by Mordig's evil," Kenric explained. "He has already struck against man once. We've barely recovered. He has also made an attempt to weaken the Fey. We are sure that the goblins will be next."

"Then góblin fight!" said Kraag. "Not scared of Mordig like puny hu-mans."

"The old lore we've been able to find says that the only way to defeat Mordig is with a true blade of power," Kenric explained.

Kraag frowned. "What old lore?"

"The lore we learned of from the Fey when we traveled to Grim Wood," Kenric said. He recited the poem that he had heard from Thulidor, the Fey smith. The words had seemed to burn themselves in his memory.

"Out of the ancient murky gloom
    Three powers arose: earth, fire, and moon.
    Each contained within a stone,
    Each is needed to keep the throne.
    United together brings strength and power,
    But twisted in evil brings our final hour."

The goblin smith was quiet when Kenric had finished. "King Orlegg has given his permission," Kenric said softly. "The smiths will be here soon. Possibly tomorrow."

"Kraag not know what hu-man and Fey smiths need!"

"Well," Kenric said, smiling as he looked around, "you're in luck. We're just the ones to help you with that."

KENRIC WAS UNABLE to sleep. They had been two full days in the goblin realm, and Kenric's father still hadn't arrived. He and Thulidor should have reached Carreg Dhu that afternoon, but they hadn't. The list of things that could have gone wrong was long. They might have been ambushed by the Sleäg or attacked by the Mawr hounds. Every time Kenric closed his eyes, new fears for his father filled his head. He rolled from his bed and began to pace.

He had done everything he could think of to gain the goblins' cooperation. So far, he had had little success. Yes, the goblin fire was critical to forging a true blade of power. The goblin smith, Kraag, seemed willing enough to help. But there was so much more the goblins could do.

Their Urgol warriors were amazingly strong. If the goblins joined with the human and Fey warriors, there was a real chance of beating Mordig. However, for all

Kenric knew, Mordig could be planning some subtler scheme. Something sneaky, like poisoning the Fey king.

"Pacing isn't going to help the time go any faster." Linwe's voice came out of the dark where she lay trying to sleep.

"Ken-ric give Hnagi headache." The little goblin scooted closer to the bubbling fire pit so Kenric wouldn't step on him.

"How can the two of you stand all this waiting?"

"What else is there to do? You've done everything you can to sway Orlegg to our side. You've driven Kraag batty with your constant questions and directions. Now we just need to—"

"Wait!" Kenric said, slapping his head in frustration. He spun around to face Linwe. "We need to talk about the kings' royal stones. We need to come up with a plan to get those back. That's what we should be doing. Not just waiting."

"What we should be doing is sleeping," said Linwe. "We can talk about that tomorr—"

A scratch at the cavern door interrupted her.

"Who's there?" Kenric called out.

Two finnboggi crept forward. Kenric thought one of them was Nuugi. "Wish to speak with Wise One,"

Nuugi said. Out of the corner of his eye, Kenric saw Linwe sit up.

Kenric looked puzzled. "Hnagi?" he asked.

Nuugi nodded.

"What Nuugi want?" Hnagi asked as he got up from his spot near the fire.

"Want to help Wise One and friends. Finnboggi can help! Know lots."

"That's probably true," Kenric said. "The other goblins act as if finnboggi are invisible."

Nuugi stepped forward and tugged on Kenric's tunic. His little head bobbed up and down. "Invisible. Yes." He took a quick look around the room, then stepped closer to Kenric. "O Great One lie," he said in a loud whisper.

"Lie?" Kenric repeated.

"Shh! Stupid hu-man! Don't tell whole realm!"

"Sorry, sorry," Kenric said, his voice much quieter. "How did the king lie?"

Nuugi threw a look at the other finnboggi, who was watching the door. "Góblin bard still live. Name Skogul. Nuugi and Glumgi take you to him. Tonight. He tell stories."

"Really?" Maybe they'd finally get some answers. "Hold on. We'll be ready in just a moment."

"Hnagi no like. What if Urgol catch?"

"Just flash them the brooch the king gave you," Kenric said as he slipped on his tunic. "They'll never know we're not on the king's business."

"It *is* the perfect opportunity," Linwe agreed.

They collected their weapons and cloaks. When they were ready, they followed Nuugi and Glumgi out into the dark hallway. "Not like this one bit," Hnagi muttered.

❧ 9 ❧

NUUGI LED THEM through the tunnels. Kenric realized he was leading them away from the main entrance. "Where are you taking us?"

"Not use front entrance. Urgol guard ask nosy questions. Go back way. Through door finnboggi use."

They turned into a large cavern. Animal carcasses were slung from the ceiling. Big, black cauldrons hung over bubbling vats of liquid fire. Finnboggi were everywhere, scrubbing out pots, skinning game, slicing meat into strips, polishing eggs. As Kenric's small group came through the kitchens, the finnboggi stopped their work and stared at Hnagi. One by one they placed their fists to their hearts. A little embarrassed, Hnagi returned the gesture.

Finally Nuugi led them into a small tunnel that reeked

of dead meat, rotten eggs, and spoiled things. Piles of garbage were stacked on either side of the narrow passageway. Kenric tried not to retch. Beside him, Linwe gagged, then covered her nose and mouth with her hand.

When they finally stumbled outside, Kenric took a giant lungful of air.

The finnboggi led them through the confusing spires of black rock and gaping caverns. Once again, Kenric became hopelessly lost. The night sky glowed faintly red from the light of the fire pits.

At last they reached a squat, lumpy-looking rock. There was a small entrance in the front of it. One of the finnboggi darted inside. He came out seconds later. "Skogul see us now. Follow Nuugi."

Ducking, Kenric followed the little goblin through a small tunnel. It opened up into a cavern. Once inside, he was relieved to find he could stand up without banging his head.

An ancient goblin scuffled forward. He was so hunched over with age that Kenric couldn't tell if he was a gurfig or an Urgol.

Nuugi introduced them. "O Wordy One, this great finnboggi that Nuugi tell Skogul about." He pointed at Hnagi. The wizened goblin crooked a finger at Hnagi.

The little goblin took a few hesitant steps forward. Skogul peered at him through milky white eyes. Next, the old goblin turned to study Linwe. "Not see Fey in long time. Almost hundred years!"

Kenric wanted to ask how old the bard was, but that seemed rude.

At last Skogul turned to Kenric. "And this is the hu-man?"

"Yes . . . sir," Kenric said. "I bring you greetings from King Thorgil and Princess Tamaril. They ask if you would share some of your stories about Mordig with us."

"Skogul know everything góblin. Mordig part of góblins' long story. Part góblin," Skogul said.

So Hnagi had been right. Mordig *was* part goblin. "But then why is he so much more powerful than the other goblins?" Kenric asked.

"Mordig is part hu-man and Fey, too," Skogul said. "Worst of all races. Twisted. Bitter. Full of hate."

The words of the prophecy came back to Kenric. *But twisted in evil brings our final hour.*

"Mordig have brute strength of góblin," Skogul continued. "Cunning of Fey and courage of man. All three."

"But how?" Kenric asked as he perched himself on a

lump of stone. "And how come the Fey and humans don't know about him?"

"But they do. Mordig father's mother was Fey princess."

Linwe gasped. "Marílla."

Kenric felt pieces of the puzzle begin to fall into place.

"Mordig's mother human queen," Skogul finished.

But the only queen Kenric could think of would have been . . . "King Thorgil's mother?" he asked.

Skogul nodded.

Kenric's head swam in confusion. "Could you tell us the whole story? From the beginning?"

The old bard settled himself on a rocky perch. "Three generations ago, twisted seed grew in góblin soil. The seed named Erdig. Erdig young góblin warrior. Strong and brave. But heart small. Not big like warrior's should be. Erdig good fighter, but not trusted. Honor tainted. Fey king, Marílla father, tell góblin king this. Góblin king listen. Not let Erdig be general, even when Erdig earn it with strength in battle.

"Erdig bitter. Slunk off to live alone. Plotted and stewed on revenge. Stole into Mithin Dûr. Kidnap Princess Marílla to punish Fey king. Erdig bring Marílla back to Helgor's Teeth. Make wife. She bore Erdig a son."

"Mordig," Kenric said, forgetting himself.

The old bard heard. "No. Not Mordig. Ilgorm. Mordig's father. Ilgorm's Fey mother scorned him. Ilgorm remind her of misery. Caught between two worlds. Accepted by none. Fey half of Ilgorm war with góblin half. When grown, Ilgorm want all to suffer like him. Kidnapped human queen for wife."

"King Thorgil's mother."

The bard nodded. "And so Mordig born. Son of góblin, son of Fey, and son of hu-man."

And half brother to King Thorgil, Kenric realized. He remembered the king insisting that his mother had been killed. Artemus had argued that she might have just been kidnapped. This meant his mother had lived long enough to have another child.

"Is that why King Orlegg resists being our ally?" Kenric asked. "Is he somehow related to Mordig?"

Skogul shrugged. "King Orlegg crafty. Try save own skin. Know Mordig did bad thing. Maybe góblin could have stopped. Maybe not. O Great One not want blame for this. Afraid to join hu-man and Fey. Then Mordig might squash him like bug. If only Prince Durrig here.

Then Orlegg not torn in two." Skogul sighed and cast a pointed look at Hnagi.

Hnagi bowed his head in shame.

"What could this Prince Durrig do?" Kenric asked.

"Prince Durrig younger. Bolder. Not crafty like King Orlegg. Have young góblin honor. Not old góblin worries."

Glumgi crept forward. "Nearly daylight. Need to get back. Not want Urgol find. Hurt finnboggi bad for disobeying."

Kenric thanked Skogul for his help. Then he followed the finnboggi back to Carreg Dhu.

Linwe nudged Kenric with her elbow. "You realize what this means, don't you? We're forging a blade of power right under the nose of someone who may be on Mordig's side."

"I know. We just have to hope he doesn't try to use it for himself."

❈ IO ❈

No SOONER HAD Kenric dropped into sleep than he was awakened by the steady rhythm of the drums. The hollow eerie sounds seemed to pound against his very heart.

"Strangers arrive," mumbled Hnagi. "Fey and human."

Kenric bolted upright. "My father and Thulidor!" As he scrambled to his feet, Linwe untangled herself from her blankets.

They raced into the large entrance chamber. Kenric's father and Thulidor stood just inside the cavern. They looked weary and dazed.

Something tight across Kenric's shoulders relaxed. He'd been so worried that something had happened to them. "Father!" he cried out, then ran across the chamber to meet him.

His father captured him in a giant bear hug. When he put Kenric down again, Kenric said, "I was afraid the Sleäg had ambushed you at Craggyness!"

"Why would you think that?"

"Because they ambushed us." Kenric told him of their adventures in the small town. Brogan's face grew grim and tight. "So, when you didn't show up yesterday afternoon," Kenric continued, "I began to worry."

"The cart slowed us down," Brogan explained.

Several finnboggi appeared just then. They gathered around the smith's cart. "Finnboggi take to forge," Nuugi said.

Kenric nodded. They began following the cart. "How is the king?" Kenric asked.

"Not well," his father told him. "He is fading into nothing but a shadow. He no longer takes food, only sips of broth now and again. I don't know how much longer he can last."

"And the princess?"

"She is as strong as steel. She will be our kingdom's strength, I think. She is gathering all the soldiers who fought under her father's command. There aren't as many as there once were. But we'll not give up without a fight."

"Cerinor, acting as regent, has put out a call to the

Fey," Thulidor added. "He sent word that Fey troops will soon be marching to Tirga Mor to lend their aid."

Linwe's eyes glowed. Kenric suspected she wanted to be there, right in the thick of battle.

"Tamaril has also called for any men who wish to volunteer. Men from as far away as Hemsby Heath are rising to our need. Even a few from Penrith. The armies are gathering," Brogan said, his eyes grim. "Tamaril hopes to have them ready to march in ten days. The Fey have guaranteed safe passage to all who must pass through Mithin Dûr. They will encamp just north of Craggyness. By the time the sword is forged, man and Fey will be ready to make their stand. Will the goblins join them?"

"Things don't look good," Kenric said. "King Orlegg will not commit to an alliance. He also lied to us about having a bard. I don't think he wanted us to find out about Mordig. But we did anyway." Kenric told them all that he had learned last night from the old bard.

When he'd finished, Brogan and Thulidor looked stunned. "So, Mordig is King Thorgil's half brother," Brogan repeated.

"Yes. He fulfills the Fey prophecy," Linwe pointed out. " 'Twisted in evil brings our final hour.' "

"I think that's why Mordig was able to bend the king's

sword to his will," Kenric told them. "Because he has the same royal blood."

"The blade must have been pulled in two different directions," Thulidor said. "Thorgil and Mordig each had an equal claim to its power. The blade shattered under the strain."

Kenric saw that they had reached the forge. "How long will it take to forge the blade of power?" Kenric asked.

"We will begin as soon as we can. We'll work fast, but these things take time."

Just then, Kraag stepped forward. The three smiths looked at one another warily. At last, the goblin smith spoke. "Come. Let me show you how real smith works." He winked at Kenric, who started to follow the smiths into the forge. Kraag stopped him. "There is much to do. Not need you under our feet."

TWO DRUMS LATER, Nuugi and Glumgi led Kenric, Linwe, and Hnagi deep into the forge. They passed the working gurfig. They passed a score of spewing liquid fire pits. When they rounded a bend in the cavern, Kenric saw an enormous fire geyser. It was the largest he'd ever seen, shooting straight up until it almost touched the rocky ceiling.

A row of finnboggi sat hidden deep within the shadows. They clasped large hide drums between their feet. As they saw the smiths approach, they began to beat on them. It was an eerie pulsing rhythm that made Kenric's whole body tense.

Kraag stepped to the head of the geyser. Kenric's father and Thulidor moved to his side.

"By the power of the earth," Brogan said. He threw a chunk of oak wood into the fire. The fire rose up, yellow-flamed and hungry.

"By the power of the moon," Thulidor said, tossing in a globe of swirling moonlight. The glass shattered. The goblin fire flared blue when it met the cold fire of the moonlight.

"By the power of the sun," Kraag said. He flung a handful of goblin dust into the geyser. It roared to life, bright orange and red flames leaping all the way to the cavern ceiling.

The drums beat faster.

Brogan placed a long piece of iron ore on the lip of the geyser. Kraag placed a strip of the strange black, glassy metal on top of that. Thulidor topped it all with a layer of Fey silver. Together, the three smiths grasped one end of the tongs holding the sword blank and thrust it into the geyser. The silver began to trickle in small bright rivulets. It mixed with the black iron ore, and the goblin metal was hidden in between.

The drums beat so fast that Kenric's skin felt as if it would rise off his bones.

At last they pulled the hot mass out of the fire. Brogan lifted his hammer and began to pound. The drumbeat shifted to match the rhythm of the hammering.

The forging of the true blade of power had begun.

⚔ II ⚔

KENRIC WAS GOING crazy. He was sure of it. The end-less waiting was making him twitchy and on edge. Try-ing to channel that energy, he renewed his focus on his sword practice.

"You've gotten better at this," Linwe said as she thrust her short sword at Kenric. He parried it easily.

"After two solid weeks of being trounced by you, I should hope so." He winced as the flat of her sword con-nected with his knuckles. The small crowd of off-duty finnboggi ooohed.

Stones' blood! He still couldn't seem to talk and fight at the same time.

While waiting for the blade to be forged, he had thrown himself into learning everything he could about fighting. He practiced swords with Linwe and wrestled with Hnagi. The little goblin had also been showing him how to throw knives. Kenric was finally beginning to feel he could defend himself.

Deciding to end this practice, he lunged forward and twisted his wrist. The sharp point of his dagger came to rest just below Linwe's throat. "Aha!" he said in triumph.

The finnboggi cheered. Linwe scowled at them. "Bah," she said, slapping his dagger away. Kenric smiled. She was always a sore loser.

Hnagi turned away from them and flicked his wrist. His sharp knife flashed through the air. It struck a leather target at the far side of the cavern with a dull *thud*. The finnboggi cheered again.

"Have you thought any more about how to retrieve the kings' bound stones?" Kenric asked Linwe. "It would be nice if we could have their power on our side when we face Mordig."

Linwe shrugged. "They won't let us out of here on our own. But I don't trust the goblin king enough to tell him what we're after."

"Neither do I," Kenric said. Orlegg still hadn't made a decision about the alliance. Kenric was growing more and more uneasy. "Perhaps it's time to check on the blade's progress again."

"And won't they just appreciate that so much," Linwe muttered as she shoved her sword into its sheath.

Kenric ignored her and slipped on his tunic. He stepped out of their cavern and strode into the hallway. After a moment, he heard Linwe and Hnagi follow.

The winding corridor took them deeper toward the heart of the mountains until they reached the goblin forge. Kenric paused at the mouth of the cavern. The place was abustle with furious activity.

Brogan glanced up and saw Kenric. He lifted his arm and wiped the sweat from his brow. His lips twitched. "I thought you were supposed to stay away from here."

Kraag looked up. "The Impatient One is back? Gah," he said, his voice thick with disgust.

Kenric felt his cheeks flush in embarrassment. "I just needed to ask how much longer until the blade will be ready."

All three smiths glared at him. He looked down at his foot and kicked a pebble. He wasn't being that much of a pest. Was he?

"It will take how long it will take," Thulidor said mysteriously.

"Yes, but we need to know so we can be ready as soon as the blade is."

Brogan looked at Thulidor. "Four days? Five?"

Kraag turned back to the fire and growled. Thulidor nodded. "Perhaps."

"Thank you," Kenric said. "We'll leave you alone now, I promise." He was distracted from his embarrassment by a deep, rapid pounding of the drums. The rhythm was urgent even to his untrained ears. It was quickly followed by a clatter of running feet that sounded like a herd of oxen stampeding.

"What are they up to now?" Kenric muttered as he stepped out into the hall. He leaped back as a solid stream of Urgol stormed by. Hnagi peeked out past Kenric's elbow. "Drums say hurry, get out of way. Important news for Great One."

"Well, let's go see what it is," Kenric said. He followed the Urgol to King Orlegg's throne room. Unnoticed in the uproar, Kenric, Linwe, and Hnagi slipped into the large cavern. One of the Urgol stepped forward and bowed low before the king. "O Great One. Sorleg brings news from northwestern perimeter."

"Speak!" Orlegg said.

"Mining party taken by Mordig. Forty finnboggi, four gurfig lost."

Orlegg's huge fist crashed down on the arm of his

throne. The wyrm at his feet reared back and hissed. Everyone froze. "Cursed Mordig keep stealing góblins! Triple perimeter guard," he ordered. "Find out who in mining party. Notify families."

Kenric's mind raced. Goblins had been captured. Perhaps King Orlegg would mount a rescue party. It might be the perfect chance to get close enough to Mordig to try to find the royal stones.

Kenric stepped forward. The wyrm turned its brilliant green eyes on him, but Kenric held his ground. "Excuse me, O Great One. But who are you going to send after the finnboggi?"

At this question, everyone in the room froze.

Orlegg swung his huge head around to stare at Kenric. "Finnboggi?"

"Yes. Who's going to rescue them?"

Orlegg scowled. "No one. Finnboggi not worth rescuing." He shrugged. "Shame about gurfig, but can't be helped."

The brutal truth of Orlegg's words struck Kenric. He turned to Hnagi, who stared at the floor. None of the finnboggi in the room would meet his gaze. With a jolt, he realized that they were ashamed. They weren't angry or mad, but embarrassed that they were so unworthy.

Injustice burned deep in Kenric's gut. "We can't just leave them there. Who knows what Mordig will do to them!"

"Use for slaves like always," the goblin king said.

Kenric took a deep breath. "Then Linwe, Hnagi, and I will travel to Mordig's lair and free the captives."

Linwe gasped. Hnagi jerked his head up to stare at Kenric.

Orlegg's eyes opened wide in surprise. "Why?" The goblin king glanced over at Hnagi. "He put you up to this?"

"No! It's just human custom to value everyone, especially prisoners of war."

"But góblin and Mordig not at war. Yet," he added.

"He crossed your borders and stole your people. Isn't that an act of war? We can't just stand by and do nothing," Kenric said. "Aren't the stronger supposed to protect the weaker?"

Hnagi sidled closer to Kenric and tugged on his tunic. "We not strong enough," the little goblin whispered.

"Not strong enough to attack Mordig's fortress," Kenric agreed. "But we're not going to do that. We're just going to slip in and free the finnboggi and the gurfig so they can escape. That's all."

Awareness dawned on Linwe's face. She smiled faintly and nodded her head.

"All we need is stealth," Kenric continued. "A small group will work better than a large one. We can hide better."

"Enough!" Orlegg shouted as he pounded his fist on the table. The wyrm rose up on its coils, ready to strike. Kenric took two steps back. "No one go anywhere." He looked directly at Kenric and pointed. "No one go unless Orlegg say. And I say no! Finnboggi not worth it."

Into the deadly quiet, Kenric spoke. "What about Prince Durrig?"

Orlegg blinked, then leaned back in his chair.

Kenric continued. "Is Prince Durrig worth rescuing? If we go in to rescue the finnboggi, we might be able to rescue him as well."

The goblin king narrowed his eyes and studied Kenric. A strange look crossed his face. It took Kenric a moment to recognize it. Hope.

"Orlegg change mind. You may go rescue finnboggi. But only if bring back Prince Durrig, too." The king turned to glare at Hnagi. "It's the least the nasty, lazy coward owe Orlegg," he said. "Orlegg command it."

Hnagi fell to his knees and bowed low to the floor so

that his forehead touched the cold stone. "Thank you, O Great One, for chance for Hnagi to regain honor."

Kenric studied the goblin king for a moment. "If we bring back your son, will you ally with us?"

"If Orlegg stand against Mordig, Mordig kill Orlegg son. But if Durrig rescued, Orlegg can fight with hu-man and Fey. Will need guide to Helgor's Teeth. Hlogg!" he bellowed.

The Urgol guard quickly appeared. "Yes, Great One?"

"Get Skrig and Gerd. Now."

"Yes, Great One." The Urgol hurried off at a trot.

The trio waited in silence. Finally Hlogg returned, leading two Urgol behind him. They bowed low in front of the king. "What does Great One wish from humble servants?" one of them asked.

"Need guide. Lead these three to Helgor's Teeth. Have a job to do for Orlegg."

One of the Urgol flicked a glance over to Hnagi. "Why not just send Skrig and Gerd? No need for finnboggi. Hnagi not deserve Orlegg's trust." The Urgol spit at Hnagi's feet. The little goblin inched back.

"Skrig question Orlegg?"

Skrig flinched, bowed his head, then shook it.

"This finnboggi earn Orlegg trust. Plus, have task to

perform." Orlegg waved his hand. "Now go. Orlegg must think."

Kenric's head reeled as he followed Gerd out of the room. These two Urgol were to be their guides. And they hated finnboggi. Hnagi especially. How did they feel about humans and Fey? he wondered.

Linwe leaned close and whispered in Kenric's ear. "Can we trust them?"

Kenric shook his head.

"What whispering?" Skrig asked. "What nasty Fey secrets you keep from Skrig and Gerd?"

"Fey and hu-man Orlegg honored guest. Treat with respect!" Hnagi's fists were clenched, and he was shaking with anger.

Not wanting Hnagi to get any angrier, Kenric stepped in. "We weren't trading secrets. Just discussing what we need to do to prepare for the journey. We should be ready to leave by first light."

"Always light in góblin realm. We leave in two drums. Be ready."

"But—" Kenric began to protest.

"Two drums," Skrig said. "Be ready."

As they stood and watched him go, Linwe turned to Hnagi. "No wonder you left the goblin realm."

⚓ 12 ⚓

THEY WERE READY in one drum. Kenric was afraid
Skrig and Gerd would be early and try to leave without
them. They were too hostile. Too anxious to see them fail.

Sure enough, Skrig showed up before the second
drum had sounded. "Ready?" he asked. He seemed dis-
appointed when he saw their packs by the door.

"Ready," said Kenric. Uneasy, he swung his pack onto
his shoulders and fell into line behind Skrig. He didn't
trust the Urgol to lead them anywhere but into trouble.

Outside, the deep gray sky was lit up with the eerie red
light, as if the entire land were on fire. Their Urgol
guides quickly picked out a path through the rocky landscape.

They spent the whole day in a blur of endless marching. Kenric hadn't realized how hardy goblins were.

They didn't need to stop for anything. Not food or water or rest. Kenric refused to be the only one to call for a halt. He kept his mouth firmly shut and marched on. He ignored the burning muscles in his legs and the gnawing hunger in his belly.

Finally the sun began to set. Vivid rays of red light spread out across the sky. In the fading light, the black rocks turned the color of dried blood.

"When do you plan to stop?" Kenric asked.

"When reach Helgor's Teeth," Skrig said.

"No. We need to stop before that."

"Puny hu-man," Gerd scoffed. "We keep marching." He turned to keep walking and nearly skewered himself on the tip of Linwe's blade.

"We want to camp here," she said. Then she shoved the tip of her sword against his belly.

Gerd howled as if he had been sliced open. "Nasty Fey blade burn!" The Urgol reached out to push it away. He put both thick hands on the blade, cutting them as he shoved the blade away from his stomach. He howled as fresh pain welled up in his cut palms. Both Urgol backed away.

"Will sleep here," Skrig agreed, staring at Linwe's blade. Then he turned to Hnagi. "Make self useful. Make camp ready, lazy finnbog—"

Linwe thrust her sword at them again.

"Hnagi is not a slave," Kenric said. "Not yours. Not ours. We will all make the camp ready."

Grumbling, the two Urgol went off to huddle by themselves.

When they were safely out of earshot, Kenric leaned in close to Linwe. "Did you know your blade would do that?"

"No. It was a happy surprise," she said, grinning. Then she scowled. "The goblin king did us no favor by giving us these two," she said as she sheathed her sword. "I don't trust them."

"I don't either. But we need to be careful not to push them into doing something we'll be sorry for."

"I think we'd be better off without them. Let's send them back."

The idea was tempting. Kenric turned to Hnagi. "Do you know the way?"

The little goblin nodded.

Kenric looked over his shoulder. "Do you think they would go back if we told them to?"

Hnagi shook his head. "That mean failed. Urgol not like to fail."

Linwe sighed. "Which means they'd probably just follow us."

"I think I'd rather have them where I can keep an eye on them," Kenric said.

Reluctantly, Linwe agreed. "That is probably wise. Annoying, but wise."

"Too bad we don't have some powerful tonics or poison we could use on them," Kenric said. "Sneaking in under Mordig's nose is hard enough. I don't want to have to be watching my back the whole time."

Linwe's eyes brightened. "Let me think a bit. Perhaps there is something we can use." She glanced at the terrain around them.

"Well, think quickly. We'll want to do it before we reach Helgor's Teeth!"

"All right. You two get some rest. I'll scout around and see if I can find anything that will knock them out."

Linwe slipped away silently. Kenric and Hnagi laid her bedroll just behind a small boulder, then rolled theirs out in front of it. Kenric thought about eating something, but before he could decide what, he was fast asleep.

KENRIC JERKED AWAKE when he felt a hand on his shoulder. "Shh! It's just me," Linwe said from somewhere close to his ear.

Kenric scrubbed his hand over his face and tried to

come fully awake. He was warm and snug in his bedroll, and sleep tugged at him. He pinched himself to fight it off.

Linwe pulled a small handful of something from her tunic. "I was in luck," she said, keeping her voice low. "I found moonwort. I wasn't sure it grew this far east, but it does. Moonwort is poisonous to goblins. It will make them weak or unconscious for several hours. Possibly even days."

Kenric glanced across the camp at the Urgol. They were fast asleep and snoring.

"Here." Linwe thrust a clump of moonwort at Kenric as he sat up. "We need to turn it into a liquid. Then we can drip it into their mouths while they sleep." She placed a small, hollowed-out stone on the ground between them. "You need to chew it, then spit it out into this. Be careful not to swallow. I don't know how moonwort affects humans." She turned to look at Hnagi, who was sitting up on his bedroll, watching. "I don't think we should let you try. It's possible it won't hurt you if you don't swallow it. But since you're a goblin, better not to take the chance."

Kenric lifted one of the leaves and studied it warily. Then he popped it into his mouth. The foul, bitter taste made his tongue curl. He chewed quickly, then gagged as he spat the pulp out onto the rock. "Does this taste good to you?" he asked Linwe.

She shrugged. "We Fey take it for medicine, so it reminds me of being sick. It's not bad, but I wouldn't want a steady diet of it."

"It's nasty." Kenric said to Hnagi. "You got off lucky this time."

Kenric and Linwe chewed for an hour until finally they had a good-size puddle of moonwort pulp.

"I had to go find the moonwort," Linwe said. "I think you and Hnagi should give it to the goblins."

"Seems fair." Kenric pushed himself to his feet, then bent over to lift the rock. He carried it carefully, not wanting to spill a drop. He headed for the sleeping Urgol with Hnagi trailing behind him.

As he approached, Skrig snorted. Kenric froze. After a long moment, the goblin began to snore again. Kenric crept closer.

He stared down at the Urgol's cruel faces. These were two he wouldn't mind poisoning. Especially since it would just make them sick and weak, not kill them.

He bent over Gerd and tilted the rock bowl toward the goblin's mouth. A thick, juicy blob of green pulp oozed from the bowl and plopped in.

Gerd's jaws snapped shut and his tongue clacked against the roof of his mouth. Kenric froze, ready to leap back if the goblin awoke. But he didn't. He just wrinkled his face up and muttered in his sleep.

Kenric quickly repeated the procedure with Skrig. This time, the glob of pulp dropped straight down the goblin's throat and he choked. Kenric and Hnagi leaped back as Skrig coughed and gurgled. But even then, he didn't wake up. He just rolled over onto his side.

They hurried back to Linwe. "I have no idea how long the moonwort will hold them," she said.

"Then we'd better get moving," Kenric said.

⚔ 13 ⚔

THE THREE OF them crouched behind a rock on the jagged ridge above Mordig's fortress. Helgor's Teeth was well named, Kenric thought. It looked like the jaws of some giant beast. The large courtyard spread out before them.

It was just past midnight. Everything was dark and mostly deserted except for a Sleäg or two. Towers and blocky stone buildings nestled at the base of the steep slope. Black caves led deep into the mountains. Iron bars covered most of the entrances.

Kenric leaned close to Hnagi. "Do you think those caves are where the prisoners are being kept?"

Hnagi nodded.

"I wonder if Prince Durrig is kept there, too, or somewhere else."

Hnagi shrugged and shook his head.

A bone-chilling snarl rose up from the courtyard. It was followed by a piercing screech. With its hackles raised, a Mawr hound growled and began circling a wyrm it had cornered against one of the tower walls. The serpentlike creature was easily twice as long as the hound. It rose up on its coils. The spikes around its neck fanned out, making it look even more terrifying.

The Mawr hound lunged, jaws snapping. The wyrm opened its mouth, displaying long, sharp fangs. There was a flash of motion. Then the two creatures quickly became a blurred tangle. The Mawr hound's great jaws clamped down on the wyrm's back. The wyrm's spiked tail thrashed angrily as it began to wrap its long body around the hound.

A Sleäg stepped forward. He pulled a whip from his belt and lashed at the fighting creatures. The wyrm hissed and reared back, then plunged forward and sank its fangs into the hound's neck.

The hound gave a piercing yelp and slumped to the ground. The Sleäg cracked the whip again, and the wyrm unwrapped itself from the hound and slithered away.

Kenric swallowed the fear that rose up in his throat. What had made him think he could pull off a rescue? Or retrieve the kings' bound stones right out from under Mordig's nose? "So," he asked, "anyone have a plan to get past the guards, the hounds, and the Sleäg?"

Linwe looked at him in disbelief. "Don't tell me you led us all the way here without a plan?"

Feeling foolish, Kenric shrugged. He opened his mouth to defend himself, but Linwe interrupted. "Is that Mordig?"

A tall, broad figure in black armor had appeared in the courtyard. Wicked spikes flared at his shoulders, wrists, and elbows. His black helm was topped with a crown of sharp, curved blades, like the horns of a wild beast. There was a slit for his mouth and two gaping holes for his eyes.

Kenric gripped the rock in front of him to keep his hands from shaking. "That's him."

Mordig strode across the courtyard. Two Sleäg hurried to keep up with him.

"Are the troops ready?" Mordig barked.

"Yes, Master," one of the Sleäg answered. "They await your command."

"Excellent. We will march on Carreg Dhu in two days' time. They should have the blade of power ready by then, and it will be mine for the taking."

One of the Mawr hounds crept toward the warlord,

crawling on its belly. Mordig kicked the hound out of the way. The great hound yelped and slunk away.

The two Sleäg glanced at each other, then slipped into the shadows. Mordig continued across the courtyard alone and disappeared into the tallest of the towers.

"Well," Kenric said, letting out a breath, "at least we know where he is. Hopefully he'll stay there until we can get the goblins free. Come on. We'll think of a plan as we go."

Kenric and the others slipped and scrambled over the rocks of Helgor's Teeth. It wasn't hard to reach the court-yard. The fortress had been designed to keep things in, not keep them out.

BY THE TIME they reached the fortress, they had a plan. No one liked it much, but it was the only thing they could come up with.

The three of them skulked between a looming tower of thick gray stone and a short, squat barracks. The alley was dark and narrow. It reeked of old carrion and other foul things.

They were waiting for a Sleäg. There had been several around earlier. But now that they needed one, none were in sight.

Kenric shifted in the darkness, then froze. He nudged Linwe. "You're *glowing*," he said.

She looked down at her arm. Now that the moon had risen, her pale skin glowed in the dark. "Sorry," she muttered.

She reached down and scooped up a handful of dirt. She quickly rubbed it over her arms and face, dulling the pale light.

Kenric settled back into his hiding place and waited. Finally a Sleäg, the one with the whip, came out of the dungeons. He strode toward a building on the far side of the compound. As he passed in front of their hiding spot, Hnagi tossed a small pebble at him.

The Sleäg turned and stared into the darkness between the buildings. "Who's there?"

The three kept quiet. Kenric clutched the three stones of power so hard his fingers ached. The Sleäg took a few steps toward them.

Closer, thought Kenric. Come closer. He wanted the Sleäg to come in all the way into the alley. That way no one in the courtyard could see what happened. Scampering back, Hnagi tossed another pebble.

The Sleäg's hand flew to his whip. He lifted it from his

belt as he strode forward. Kenric gripped the stones harder to keep his hands from shaking.

Farther, farther . . . There!

Just then, the Sleäg tripped over something in the dark. His whip flew from his hand, and he went sprawling onto the ground face-first. Immediately Kenric spoke the words. "By the power of the earth, moon, and fire, I bind you with these stones as they are bound to my king's will. Show yourself!"

The Sleäg began to twist and squirm. Foul gray mist began to rise from its writhing body. Kenric covered his nose and waited for the night breeze to carry the mist away. In the distance, the Mawr hounds began their hideous gibbering. Squawking and rustling noises came from somewhere behind them. Kenric glanced over his shoulder. "What's that racket?"

Linwe and Hnagi crept from their hiding places, where they'd held the rope for the Sleäg to trip over. "I don't know. Do you think the hounds sensed the magic?" Linwe asked.

"Yes. But what's that behind us?"

Linwe slipped away into the darkness, then reappeared seconds later. "Grymclaws," she said. "Their cage

is right behind us. They must have felt the magic, too."
She stepped closer to the Sleäg. "Is he dead?"

"I don't know," said Kenric. "Your father didn't die
when this happened to him. But then, he wasn't nearly as
far gone. The only other time I've seen this was on a
Sleäg who was badly wounded. I don't know if he died
from his wounds or the . . . stuff leaving his body." He
took a deep breath. "Well, there's no point in waiting."
Gingerly, he rolled the Sleäg over. He unfastened the
creature's cloak, trying hard to keep his fingers from
touching the limp form.

Hnagi reached into one of his pouches. He pulled out
a handful of his goblin dust. Kenric was surprised to see
it looked just like ashes. The little goblin rubbed them on
his face. When he was done, Linwe pulled a piece of
charcoal from her pocket. She glanced down at the fallen
Sleäg, then leaned in toward Hnagi. She smudged dark
shadows around his eyes and mouth. "There," she said.
"With the whiteness of the ashes and the shadows I've
drawn, you look just like a Sleäg now."

Hnagi hissed. "Don't say that!"

"Come on, Hnagi," Kenric called out softly. "I'm
ready."

The goblin scuttled over to Kenric, who lifted him

onto his shoulders. Hnagi settled himself as if he were getting a piggyback ride.

"Okay, Linwe. Help us with the cloak."

She helped Kenric drape the long black cloak around himself and Hnagi. She reached up to fasten it around Hnagi's neck, making sure it gaped open enough in front that Kenric could see where he was going.

"The whip," he reminded her. Linwe found the Sleäg's whip and handed it to Kenric. She pulled the hood up close around Hnagi's face.

"The disguise isn't bad," she told him. "If you keep the hood up, no one can see you're a goblin."

Kenric shuddered. "It gives me the shivers. I hate parading around in something a Sleäg has worn."

"Well, there is that," Linwe agreed. "I'll wait for you here. Don't take too long."

"If we're not back, or it looks like we're in trouble, don't stick around. Get back to the goblin realm as quickly as you can. The last thing we need is for Mordig to have another hostage."

Linwe rolled her eyes.

"Promise!"

"I promise," she huffed out. "But I'll see you and your herd of finnboggi before long. I'm sure of it."

Kenric nodded, then turned and walked toward the courtyard. Hnagi was surprisingly heavy for someone so small.

The goblin wobbled and bobbed on his shoulders as they approached the dungeons. Hopefully, any guards would recognize the cape and the whip and let them through. That was their plan anyway.

The closer he got to the dungeon, the more Kenric disliked the plan.

❧ 14 ❧

KENRIC TOOK LONG steps, trying to walk like a Sleäg. It was hard because Hnagi's weight kept him off balance. As they approached the entrance to the dungeon, the goblin guard stood up. "Forget something?" he asked, unlocking the gate.

Kenric felt Hnagi shake his head.

"What need then?" the guard asked.

Kenric said nothing but used the whip to point toward the prison.

"But just here," the goblin said, puzzled.

Kenric took two more steps toward him.

"Who are you?" the goblin asked, his voice rising.

Peering through the gap in his cloak, Kenric lashed out with the whip. Before the guard knew what was happening, Kenric wound it tightly around his neck.

The guard clutched at his throat and made a gurgling noise.

"Squeeze tight," Hnagi ordered. "Be sure nasty góblin good and dead."

"No!" Kenric said with a final squeeze. "I just want him unconscious, not dead." He grabbed the keys from the guard's belt as he eased him to the ground.

Kenric stepped over the fallen guard into the cave. The stench of too many unwashed bodies in a close place smacked him in the face. Rows of cages lined the cavern walls. They were full of hundreds of bedraggled finnboggi. Kenric pushed their misery out of his mind before it paralyzed him. He was here to help, he reminded himself. Soon they would be free. He reached the first cage and found the lock.

Murmuring, all the finnboggi backed away.

"We're here to help. Don't be afraid," Kenric said, struggling with the rusty lock. When it finally sprang open, the finnboggi shrank back from him. "Really! It's okay."

One little finnboggi shook his head. "Not trust Sleäg."

He'd forgotten his disguise! Quickly he reached up and lifted Hnagi from his shoulders. All the finnboggi gasped. Kenric realized it must look like he was removing his own head. He set Hnagi on the ground, and the finnboggi crowded forward. "Finnboggi?" one of them asked in wonder.

Hnagi nodded. "Finnboggi and hu-man come to help. Free all finnboggi. Hurry." He pulled Kenric to the next pen. Kenric unlocked it, and more finnboggi spilled into the cavern. When he unlocked the third pen, he asked the first finnboggi who came out, "Where are they keeping Prince Durrig?"

"Not know," the finnboggi said, then hurried to join the others. As more and more of them were freed, their voices rose in excited chatter.

"Shh!" Hnagi whispered at them.

Kenric opened the last pen. "Do any of you know where they're keeping Prince Durrig? We have to free him, too."

One of the finnboggi nodded and pointed to the back of the cavern.

"Can you show me?"

He nodded again and led Kenric and Hnagi to a small, dank cell. It was all closed in, with a solid door that had only a small opening. It reminded Kenric of the prison cell where he'd found his father.

"Prince Durrig? Are you in there?" Kenric whispered.

There was a rattle of chains. "Who's there?" a weak voice called out.

"We're here to free you."

It took Kenric a minute to find the right key for the door. When he finally opened it, a young Urgol shuffled out. His hands and feet were bound with chains. "Prince Durrig?"

The goblin nodded warily. He spied Hnagi off to Kenric's left. "You?"

Hnagi threw himself down on the prison floor, face-first. "Hnagi beg pardon, O Princely One. Never meant to leave you to rot in Mordig prison. Hnagi hope to earn pardon."

The prince looked at Hnagi in surprise. "Hnagi not need Durrig pardon," he said. "Not do anything wrong."

Hnagi wriggled on the floor. "Hnagi should die to save you."

"And waste two lives?" Prince Durrig asked.

Hnagi rose from the floor, but his face was still worried. The prince put his hand on Hnagi's bowed head. "Hnagi have Durrig pardon, even though nothing to forgive. But what Hnagi doing here?"

"It's a long story," Kenric said.

Prince Durrig looked at Kenric as if he'd forgotten he was there. "What hu-man doing here?"

"I am Kenric of Penrith. I was sent by King Thorgil to try to convince your father to ally himself with Fey and man against Mordig. Rescuing you was the only way he would agree," Kenric said as he knelt to study the prince's manacles.

"Shames Durrig that a hu-man rescue him when góblins not. Ken-ric have Durrig's thanks. How can Durrig repay?"

"By making sure your father keeps his promise," Kenric said. As he began searching through the keys, he filled Durrig in on all that had happened.

"But for now you need to get back to Carreg Dhu as fast as you can," Kenric said as he found a likely key. He bent toward the Prince's feet. "You should be safe once you cross the borders. Your father has tripled the perimeter guard."

"Wrong one," Kenric muttered when the key didn't work. He groped for another. "When you reach the goblin realm, you must make your way to the smiths. Tell them to bring the sword to the ward stone. Mordig is on the move."

Kenric looked up into Durrig's eyes. "Don't let your father delay. They must meet us at the ward stone as soon as they can."

Durrig nodded, solemn. "Hu-man free me from nightmare. Hu-man free finnboggi. Have good heart. Durrig trust. Will make Great One keep promise."

"Tell Great One about Hnagi's pardon, too," the little goblin chimed in.

"But first we need to get you out of these chains." Still kneeling, Kenric tried the last key. "Stones' blood! None of these keys work." They were running out of time.

"Stones," Hnagi whispered to him. "Use stones."

"But what if the power attracts attention?"

"No choice."

The goblin was right. Kenric sighed and pulled the stones from his pocket. He held them out to the manacles that bound the goblin prince. "By the power of the earth, moon, and fire, I bind you with these stones as they are bound to my king's will. Release him!"

There was a blinding flash and crackle. The manacles snapped free as if they had been split by some invisible ax. Outside, the Mawr hounds howled.

Prince Durrig raised his fist to his heart and thumped it once. "Will do as Ken-ric commands."

"No, no! It's not a command. More like a plan . . ." His words stumbled to a halt. One by one, the other goblins, even the gurfig, raised their fists to their hearts. Kenric blinked, unsure what to say.

"Think they like you," Hnagi murmured.

"Th-thank you," Kenric said to the goblins. "Now come on! We've got to get out of here. Before we're trapped inside."

Kenric and Hnagi started flapping their hands at the goblins, trying to get them moving. "If we don't get out of here, you'll all get put back in your pens. Mordig will punish you!" Kenric said.

Prince Durrig stepped to the front of the cave. "Brave finnboggi," he called out.

Immediately they grew quiet.

"Finnboggi have shown Durrig honor and bravery. Without you, Durrig surely die in Mordig's prison. Now have chance to show all of góblin realm how brave finnboggi are. Show them your honor and strength. Come. Must hurry. Warn others about Mordig's army so no góblin will ever rot in his prison again!"

The finnboggi thumped their fists to their chests one more time. Then they moved toward the door, picking up speed. Kenric knew they would be most vulnerable as they made their way across the courtyard. Once they reached the cover of the mountains, they could scatter. Hopefully that would throw Mordig off their trail. Or at least confuse him.

Prince Durrig stopped in front of Kenric. "Not coming?"

"No. We have one more thing we must do."

"What else worth risking life for?"

Kenric felt he could trust the prince. "Mordig has stolen two royal stones. He has the Fey king's moonstone and the human king's bloodstone."

Prince Durrig paled. "That explain it."

"Explains what?"

"Mordig power. Has three royal stones. Give him power."

"Three?" Kenric asked, confused.

"Mordig take Durrig's bound firestone when first captured. Not king's stone. But still bound to royal family."

Kenric felt a tug on his cape. Hnagi was staring up at him. "Must hurry," the little goblin urged.

"You're right." Kenric looked back up at the prince. "Good luck."

"And to you," the prince said. "Durrig make sure Great One do what you ask." Then the prince turned and followed the finnboggi out of the cave.

❖ 15 ❖

OUTSIDE, KENRIC STARED at the black tower where they'd last seen Mordig. He jumped when he heard Linwe's voice near his ear. "I don't like this. Once we're inside, Mordig will have us trapped!"

"Weren't you supposed to wait for us back there?"

She shrugged. "I couldn't stand the stink of the grym-claws any longer."

Kenric looked at her in disbelief. "When did you get so fussy?"

"Oh, all right! I couldn't stand to see them locked up like that. Are you satisfied now?"

Kenric smiled. "Yes," he said. "Now, can you think of a way to get what we need without going into that tower?"

"No."

"Then we have no choice." Keeping to the shadows,

Kenric led them toward the tower. "You and Hnagi can stay here. I'll go inside alone," he said. Linwe and Hnagi whispered furiously. A moment later, Linwe appeared at his side. "I'm coming with you. Hnagi will keep watch by the entrance."

Taking a deep breath, Kenric stepped into the tower. There was no sign of Mordig or guards or even servants. They inched along the stone walls. Soon they came to a stairway leading up and a corridor leading down.

"Stones' blood!" Kenric said. "Now what?"

"There are only two ways he could have gone," Linwe pointed out. "Up those stairs or through that door. Pick one."

Kenric strained to listen for signs of life, but heard none. "The stairs," he said at last. It was late. Sleeping chambers were usually on the higher floors, not down below.

At the top of the stairs, a large balcony wound in a half circle. Kenric stepped out onto it, his eyes focused on the door at the far end.

Linwe's hand clamped down on his elbow and jerked him back. "Look," she said.

Peering through the stone railing, Kenric saw Mordig pacing in the chamber below. Kenric sucked in a breath when he saw the second figure in the room. The creature was twisted and misshapen, with pointed yellow teeth. His nose seemed to grow in one direction, his chin in another. One ear faced forward, the other twisted back. "Who is that?" he asked Linwe, keeping his voice low.

Linwe shook her head.

The shriveled figure stepped forward to take Mordig's cloak from his shoulders. "Were you able to get any word out of the newest captives?" he asked.

"None. If the goblin king is planning anything, these goblins don't know it."

"Did you persuade them hard enough? In my day—"

"You dare question me?" Mordig thundered as he turned on the creature.

"A thousand pardons." The creature bobbed and scurried to hang up the cloak.

As Mordig stood without his cloak, Kenric saw an amulet with three stones hanging around his neck. Of course! Why hadn't he thought of that before? Mordig must have a bound stone. If they could take it from him, surely it would weaken the warlord. There had to be some way to use it against him.

The twisted creature glanced sideways at Mordig. "There are interesting goings on in the góblin realm. The drums speak of Fey and man coming this way." He said this as if he were offering Mordig a great prize.

"Bah! My spies reported this days ago. In fact, they are bringing the Fey and human to me even as we speak."

Kenric and Linwe stared at each other with wide eyes. Skrig and Gerd! They were Mordig's spies! Suddenly their hostility made sense.

"What do you plan to do with them?"

"I will use them as hostages. One of them is the son of the smith who is working on the blade of power. I am fairly sure the Fey girl is the Princess Linwe. Once the blade of power is finished, I will allow the alliance to make a trade. In exchange for the sword, I will return Prince Durrig, the smith's boy, and the Fey princess to them."

"So it began with a princess, and it ends with a princess," the creature said, staring off into the distance. He turned back to the warlord. "Do you think they will trade? Would they really be so soft? So stupid?"

"I have dealt with them for five years now. They *are* that soft and that stupid."

"So we truly hold the whole kingdom of Lowthar within our grasp. You have done well, my son."

My son? Kenric mouthed at Linwe. That twisted creature was Mordig's father! Ilgorm, the goblin bard had called him.

Mordig whirled on his father, who cringed. "*I* hold the kingdom of Lowthar in my grasp. Not you." He thrust his hands at his father. The older man flinched, then reached out to unbuckle Mordig's wrist guards. Kenric swallowed a gasp and nudged Linwe. In the middle of each black metal wrist guard sat a stone. A large blood-stone in the right, a large moonstone in the left. The two kings' royal stones.

Mordig pulled the guards from his wrists and tossed them toward the wall. As they clattered into a chest, there was a sharp hissing sound. Kenric peered through the gloom and saw an enormous wyrm wrapped around the chest.

"I've had enough of your prattle, old man. Leave me."

His father bowed low, then left the room.

Kenric motioned for Linwe to follow him. They re-traced their steps out into the hallway.

"Mordig's stones!" Kenric whispered. "Those must be his bound stones in the amulet around his neck."

"Three of them?" Linwe asked.

"If he's really all three races, it makes sense. But think. If we can get those, we'll have a much better chance.

We should be able to use them against him somehow."

"But just how do you propose to get them?" Linwe asked.

"Maybe he'll take them off when he goes to sleep," Kenric suggested hopefully.

"No one takes off their bound stone," Linwe scoffed. "Not even to sleep."

"Well, I'll try to think of something."

"Let's stick to our original plan for now," Linwe said. "We need those two stones from his wrists. Those are the ones we came for."

"What do we do about the wyrm?"

"I've been thinking about that. I'll creep to the far side of the room and draw the wyrm's attention. While he's focused on me, you can grab the stones from the chest and slip back out."

"Where will Mordig be this whole time?"

"Hopefully sleeping. Surely even he sleeps sometimes."

"I wouldn't be so sure," Kenric said, watching the pacing warlord. "But it's the best idea we've got." They watched and waited for what seemed like forever. Finally Mordig threw himself into a chair by the fire. It wasn't long before his head nodded to his chest.

Kenric and Linwe slipped back out onto the balcony.

Not wanting to risk being seen, they lowered themselves to their stomachs and crawled. They finally reached the far side and crept down the stairs into Mordig's chamber. Linwe dodged around the back to the other side of the room. Kenric clung to the shadows of the stairs.

The chest with the stones was only a few yards away. The good news was that Mordig had his back to it. The bad news was that the big wyrm was still coiled tightly around it.

Kenric watched as Linwe slipped into her position across the room. Slowly, his nerves aprickle with dread, he inched his way toward the chest.

A log fell in the fireplace. Kenric froze, but Mordig only stirred in his chair. Perhaps he truly was asleep.

When Kenric was within a few feet of the chest, Linwe motioned to him to stop. He had no idea how she planned to get the wyrm's attention without alerting Mordig. Once she did, they'd have to move fast. Bracing himself, Kenric stood at the ready.

In the light of the fire, Kenric saw Linwe toss something toward the wyrm. It hit the creature on the nose. The wyrm's eyes shot open, and its mouth gaped in a silent hiss. It raised its head.

Another object bounced off the wyrm's back. The

wyrm rose up on its coils. Kenric was shocked to see it was more than twice as long as he was tall. It could almost reach Linwe without moving away from the chest.

The wyrm lunged forward, searching the shadows for the disturbance. Kenric made his move. Stepping over the wyrm's tail, he snatched the two wrist guards out of the chest. The clink of metal broke the silence, and Kenric winced. The wyrm's head whipped toward him. The beast hissed again, this time sending a small stream of fire in Kenric's direction. He turned and raced for the stairs.

A sharp, burning pain stabbed through his left arm. The wyrm had bitten him! He staggered and looked over his shoulder to see it draw back for another strike. In the darkness, Linwe's silver blade flashed.

The wyrm screeched in agony as her sword stabbed into its flesh. As it turned on Linwe with opened jaws, Mordig sprang from his chair. Kenric scrambled up the stairs.

White-hot pain pulsed in his arm. He was dizzy and half afraid he was going to be sick. Linwe appeared at his side. She grabbed him and pulled him along behind her.

Mordig's bellow of rage followed them up the stairs.

❈ 16 ❈

THEY RACED ACROSS the balcony and down the far stairs. Kenric's feet didn't seem to be working properly. They kept getting tangled up.

They reached Hnagi waiting by the door. "Run!" Linwe called out to him as they raced by.

She paused at the door long enough to peer into the courtyard and make sure no one was there. They scurried around the back of the tower toward the mountains. The sun was just beginning to rise.

From somewhere behind them, another bellow rang out. The courtyard sprang to life, shouts and orders flying through the air.

"Hurry," Linwe said. "We've got to get through this gorge before they block it off."

"Coming," Kenric huffed. His throat felt tight, and he

was having a hard time breathing. He blinked the sweat out of his eyes and staggered after Linwe.

She led them around the corner of the tower and down a narrow passageway. Without warning, she shoved Kenric flat against the wall. A score of guards trotted past the alley.

Pressed against the cold stone, Kenric fumbled with his pack, trying to put Mordig's wrist guards in. Then he closed his eyes, just for a moment. His head was thudding, and his body felt as if it were on fire.

"Ken-ric all right?" Hnagi asked.

Kenric opened his eyes and saw the little goblin peering up at him. Kenric opened his mouth to answer, but his tongue wouldn't work.

"What is wrong with you?" Linwe asked, impatient. She grabbed his shoulder to shake him. Kenric cried out as pain stabbed through him. It was so fierce he nearly passed out.

Linwe jerked her hand away and stared at his upper arm. "You were bitten! By that wyrm!"

"Wyrm bite?" Hnagi asked, scowling. "Wyrm bite poison for hu-mans. And Fey."

Kenric's mind grabbed at the word *poison*. He could barely make out the rest of what Hnagi was saying.

"Come on," Linwe said. "We need to get him out of here." She grabbed Kenric's good arm and pulled him toward the shelter of the mountain passes. "Is there a cure for wyrm bites?" she asked Hnagi.

"Yes, but take time. Quiet place."

"How much time do we have before . . . before it's too late?"

"Five drums. Maybe more. Once Ken-ric's tongue turn black, have to move fast."

"Well, come on, then. We need to get him someplace where you can take care of him."

"Me?" Hnagi squealed.

"Yes, you!" Linwe said. "You don't think I know anything about wyrm bites, do you? Now hurry!"

ON FIRE. KENRIC was certain his whole body was on fire. Flames ran through his veins instead of blood. Sweat poured from his body. No sooner did he wipe it away from his brow than it was back again. When he looked up, the world was a maze of rocky spires and misshapen stone. Rocky hills appeared out of nowhere. Kenric found himself being half pushed, half pulled up their slopes.

His mouth was so dry that he could feel his lips and tongue beginning to crack. His feet would barely walk.

His legs felt as if they were filled with lead. He stared at the ground before him, focusing on putting one foot in front of the other. He had no idea where they were or where they were going.

They stopped for a moment, and words floated by like clouds on a breeze. "He can't last much longer."

"Check his tongue."

Kenric felt sharp pincers grab his swollen tongue and yank on it. "Not black yet. Still have time. Must find someplace safe."

". . . just have to risk it . . ."

Then Kenric was pulled and shoved forward again. It was all he could do to stay on his feet. His head grew lighter and lighter until he was half afraid it would float away.

Kenric had no idea how much longer he stumbled through the black rocky landscape. The world grew dim. It was as if everything were covered in soft gray mist. His legs were numb now, and he kept falling to his knees. Something—or someone—jerked him to his feet. Then everything began spinning faster and faster until the whole world went black.

The sound of voices reached him. "Hold still," a soft

voice said. "Hnagi is going to use the firestone to try and draw the poison from the bite."

Poison? Kenric thought. What poison? And who is Hnagi?

Then his arm erupted in pain. It felt as if hot iron was being shoved into his shoulder. He bucked and rolled, trying to get away.

But arms and hands held him firm. "By the moon! Hold still, you fool! We're trying to save you."

The burning pain grew sharper and sharper. It felt as if the only thing left of Kenric's body was that one ago- nizing place. It began to throb and pulse. The pain gath- ered in his arm, then burst out. Kenric could see the swirling mass of blue and orange even from behind his closed lids. Slowly, his body began to cool.

"Got it."

"You're sure?"

"Hnagi sure. Look. Ken-ric's face better." Kenric felt someone grip his tongue again and yank it out. "Tongue pink again. All better."

"What are you doing?" Kenric asked, embarrassed when his voice croaked.

"Hnagi is curing you of that wyrm bite," Linwe said as

she peered down at him. Slowly, her face came into focus.

"So that's why I feel as if I've been hammered against an anvil," Kenric said.

"Most likely."

Kenric was silent for a moment, trying to collect his thoughts. "Where are we? How long has it been since we left Helgor's Teeth?"

"Almost a day and a half," Linwe said. "At first we went southeast to let the pursuers think we were returning to Carreg Dhu. We marched half a day in that direction. Next we veered southwest toward the ward stone. You were barely conscious the whole time. Finally you got so bad you couldn't walk. We had to find someplace Hnagi could treat you."

"Hnagi never treat wyrm bite before," the little goblin said, scooting close to Kenric.

Linwe looked at him curiously. "Then how did you know what to do?"

Hnagi shrugged. "All góblin *know*. Hnagi just never do before. How Ken-ric feel?" he asked.

"Better, but still weaker than a baby bird. So where are we now?"

"We picked out a high rocky ledge with some cover,"

Linwe told him, scanning the horizon. "We're keeping a lookout for anyone following us. So far, we haven't seen anything."

"Well, that's good. I'm sorry to have slowed you down so badly."

Linwe shrugged. "It couldn't be helped. It's not as if you asked to be bitten by the wyrm."

"How long does it take to recover from a wyrm bite?" Kenric asked Hnagi.

"Days," the little goblin said.

"We don't have days," Linwe said, her face drawn with worry.

"I'll be ready to march again soon," Kenric said. "I just need a few more hours' rest."

Linwe's face brightened. "Hnagi and I could use some rest, too. You're a heavy thing to lug around, let me tell you."

They took turns sleeping, with one of them always on watch. By the time it was Kenric's turn, his body already felt refreshed and stronger. He was heartened that they hadn't seen any signs of their pursuers. Maybe they'd lost them.

A clink of stone sounded in the darkness. Kenric

froze. There was another clink. He inched forward on his belly until he reached the edge of the plateau.

Below, goblins were spilling out of a hole in the base of the next hill over, like ants pouring out of their nest. There were half a dozen taller figures with them. Sleäg.

Mordig's search party had found them.

❧ 17 ❧

KENRIC HURRIED TO wake Hnagi and Linwe. "They've found us. Come on, we have to leave now."

The Fey and the goblin rose groggily to their feet.

"By the moon!" Linwe said. "I thought we'd lost them. How'd they track us so well?"

Hnagi pointed to his nose and sniffed.

"I'd forgotten about that," Kenric admitted.

"Plus góblin not walk like turtles. Góblin march-run. Travel twice as fast as injured Ken-ric."

They rushed to their escape route on the far side of the hill.

A score of goblins were making their way up the side. "Stones' blood!" Kenric swore.

They fanned out around the hilltop and quickly saw they were surrounded. "Now what?" Hnagi asked.

Kenric looked at him, then at Linwe. He refused to accept that this could be the end. "Now we fight."

Linwe gave a tight smile.

"But whatever we do, we can't let them take us. Hopefully they have orders to capture us alive. Then we can be traded for the blade. That will give us an advantage because we don't care how much we hurt them."

Just then, Linwe lunged past Kenric, pulling her sword from its sheath. She brought it down hard on a thick, knobby arm that clung to the mountaintop. There was a shriek, and the arm disappeared. The three of them tried to defend their position. They covered as much of the perimeter as they could. How long they slashed and struck, Kenric had no idea. No sooner would he cut at one hairy arm when another would take its place. There were just too many of them.

"Sleäg coming up," Linwe called out.

"Here, too," Hnagi said.

Kenric blinked the sweat out of his eyes. A Sleäg was steadily making its way up the slope in front of him as well. As their eyes met, the Sleäg gave a smile that made Kenric shudder.

"The stones!" he called to the others. "I'm going to use the stones against the Sleäg."

He quickly sheathed his long knife and grabbed the pouch of stones. He hoped it would work on more than one of them at a time.

"By the power of the earth, moon, and fire, I bind you with these stones as they are bound to the king's will. Show yourself."

The Sleäg in front of him fell to the ground.

"He's down!" Linwe called from her position.

"Here, too," Hnagi called back.

Kenric watched the Sleäg begin to squirm and writhe. The goblins stopped climbing and watched, fear on their faces.

The trio backed away from the edge to stand back-to-back. "Now what?" Linwe asked. "How do we use this to our advantage? The goblins will still fight."

"I don't know," Kenric said. "I hadn't thought that far."

There was a shriek in the air, answered by another shriek.

"Power of stones call nasty grymclaw," Hnagi scolded. Kenric looked up into the night sky. Hnagi was right. A flock of grymclaws was heading straight for them.

"Take cover!" Kenric shouted.

"I'm not sure we need to," Linwe said.

"We don't have time to argue about this now," Kenric said.

"I don't think they'll be a problem," Linwe said.

"What do you mean?"

"I got restless while I was waiting for you to free the finnboggi. I realized I could do a few things to help our chances."

"Like what?"

"Like freeing all the grymclaws. I think they are here to hel—"

Her words were cut off as the lead grymclaw swooped down and snagged the Fey girl off the rocks. Kenric's jaw dropped as Linwe dangled from the grymclaw's talons.

There was a swoosh of wings behind him. Before he even had time to think, he felt a jerk as long talons dug into his pack. The ground fell away, and he found himself rising up into the night sky. A third grymclaw carried Hnagi.

Kenric wanted to fight, but feared that the giant bird would drop him. In the pale red light of the night, he saw the jagged peaks of Helgor's Teeth.

But the grymclaw wasn't heading that way.

Linwe's grymclaw drew closer to his. The Fey girl was smiling from ear to ear. "They *are* here to help! They felt the flash of your magic and used that to find us. They will carry us wherever we want to go."

Kenric was speechless.

"I told you they weren't horrible creatures. Where do you want them to take us?"

"To the ward stone."

❧ 18 ❧

THE WARD STONE sat at the point where all three realms met. Carried high above the earth in the grymclaw's talons, Kenric could see a clearing. In the pale moonlight, he could make out the rugged mountains to the north, behind them. Grim Wood loomed in the west. Off to the south lay the gentle rolling fields of man. In the middle of the clearing rose three columns. One of them glowed faintly. Then Kenric's stomach wobbled as the grymclaw swooped in to land.

The grymclaws set them down beside the three pillars of stone. They thanked the grymclaws, then bid them good-bye. Filled with awe, Kenric walked over to the ward stone. Linwe and Hnagi followed.

The three columns towered above Kenric. The moonstone pillar glowed like a beacon when Linwe stroked it. The firestone pillar had streaks of orange and red swirling in its depths. The third pillar, the bloodstone, looked nearly black in the dark. Unable to resist, Kenric reached out and touched the bloodstone. Bright red drops sprang to life up and down the huge column. He could feel the pure power pulsing through it. His skin tingled just the way it did before a thunderstorm.

He turned to Linwe, his voice filled with wonder. "What exactly *are* the ward stones, anyway?"

"According to Cerinor, back when the world was first formed, there were three powers—earth, moon, and fire. But these three elements soon realized that their power would tear apart this new world. So they agreed to withdraw, each to a new realm, for the greater good of their world. They would leave only a token of their powers behind. Fire chose the daytime sky, and the moon chose the nighttime sky. Earth was content with the world below, and formed herself beneath our feet.

"As a reminder of their sacrifice, just before they changed themselves, they erected the ward stone. One pillar of luna-lith, one of igni-lith, and one of blûd-lith. When the earth, moon, and fire finally cast themselves from this world, they left scattered bits of themselves behind."

"The stones," Kenric said.

"Exactly. Now come on," Linwe said, her voice barely a whisper. "Let's find someplace to rest."

They found a spot just behind the bloodstone pillar. Kenric let himself collapse onto the ground. His arm ached, and he felt surprisingly weak. Hnagi and Linwe flopped down next to him.

"This whole task has gone much worse than I ever imagined," Kenric said.

"It's not over yet," Linwe said.

"I know. That's what worries me. We have no way of knowing if the finnboggi made it back to Carreg Dhu in time. Or if Prince Durrig was able to convince Orlegg to join the alliance. We can only hope that the smiths are on their way here with the blade."

"Finnboggi reach in time," Hnagi said. It was the first time he'd spoken since their rescue by the grymclaws. His voice was full of certainty.

"How can you be so sure?" Linwe asked.

"Finnboggi strong. Fast. Will march double time. Finnboggi honor Hnagi. Honor Kenric. Will not fail.

Plus, Prince Durrig promise. Prince Durrig never lie."

The little goblin's words gave Kenric some comfort. "Well, that's good, then. Now all we have to worry about is Orlegg, the sword, and Mordig."

They stopped talking, and Kenric drifted into his own thoughts. "Do you think Lowthar stands a chance?" he asked.

Linwe was quiet a long time before she finally answered. "Not without the blade of power. Our fighting forces are too few in number."

"Well, we'll just have to hope we get the blade in time," Kenric said. He took a deep breath and forced the grim thoughts from his mind.

WITH A START, Kenric came awake. He hadn't meant to nod off. He blinked and looked around. The moon was low in the sky. The night felt lonely and still, as if it were holding its breath. What had awakened him? he wondered, peering out into the darkness.

He heard a quiet rasp of movement across the ground. He quickly nudged Linwe and Hnagi awake. When he turned back, he saw forces gathering on the far side of the clearing. It was hard to tell in the dark. It looked like goblins and Sleäg standing alongside Mawr hounds and wyrms. There were other creatures that Kenric couldn't quite make out.

The army parted, and a tall figure strode out. His black armor seemed to absorb every speck of light around him. Mordig.

"I know you're there." The warlord's harsh voice rang out through the darkness. "I can smell your fear."

Despite all their attempts to trick him, he had known they would come here. And he'd reached them before the blade of power had. Their only hope would be to try to take Mordig's bound stones from him. Try to lessen the warlord's power. Kenric's gaze flew to Mordig's chest. He was afraid the stones would be hidden under his armor. But no, the amulet with the three stones was in plain sight. At least one thing was going their way.

"Did your king really think to threaten me with children?" Mordig asked. "What a doddering old fool. No wonder Lowthar is ripe for the plucking."

Kenric clenched his hands into fists. "King Thorgil is a good king. And he's your brother! How can you treat him so badly?"

"Some of the same blood flows in our veins, that is all. That does not make him my brother. He is my enemy. If he deserved Lowthar, he would not have lost it so easily. Now he will fall. For good this time, since you have so thoughtfully forged a true blade of power for me. Now, I think you have some things of mine," Mordig said. "I want them back." He waved a gloved hand. Two Sleäg came forward.

Kenric knew his knife was useless against their power. He fumbled in his pocket for the stones. When the Sleäg were close enough, Kenric pulled the stones from his pocket. "By the power of the earth, moon, and fire, I bind you with these stones as they are bound to the king's will. Show yourself."

A sharp crack rang out. Pain bit into Kenric's hand. He looked down, surprised to see the end of a whip wrapped around his fingers. He glanced up and saw Mordig holding the whip.

"I was hoping you'd bring those out to play. I want them. Then you will be mine." Mordig's eyes burned from behind his helm.

"W-what are you talking about?" Kenric tried to keep his voice steady. "They're not bound to me. They won't give you any power over me."

"Fool!" Mordig laughed. "You have called on their power. Many times. That in itself binds you to the stones!"

Kenric shook his head, not wanting to believe the warlord's words. If he was truly bound to the stones, then Mordig *would* use them against him.

"Now," Mordig said as he stepped over the fallen Sleäg. "When your softhearted smiths bring you the true blade of power, I will order you to hand it over. I won't have to do a thing. You will bring your kingdom to me."

The full force of Mordig's words sank in. The warlord could make Kenric hand over the Blade of Lowthar. Force him to betray his country, his friends, his family. Horror spread through him, clouding his mind, weakening his limbs. Mordig tugged on the whip, dragging Kenric forward.

Kenric caught a flicker of movement out of the corner of his eye. It was Hnagi, creeping behind the ward stones toward the warlord.

Silver flashed on Kenric's right as Linwe's sword slashed down on the whip. The bright blade severed the tie between Kenric and the warlord. Kenric reeled back as his arm jerked free. He found he was able to breathe again.

"You'll pay for that," Mordig said, turning his attention to Linwe.

"Son!" Kenric heard his father's voice and looked over his shoulder. Thulidor, Kraag, and his father stood just beyond the pillar of bloodstone. They'd made it! With the sword!

Just then, Mordig bellowed.

Kenric looked back. Hnagi was attached to the warlord's back like a cocklebur. Mordig spun around, trying to dislodge the goblin. The warlord reached up to pluck Hnagi off. The goblin's fingers wrapped around Mordig's amulet. Kenric could hear Hnagi's hiss of pain as the moonstone scorched his fingers. The little goblin jerked the chain from the warlord's neck. Just as Mordig's hand clamped around the goblin, he threw the stones to Kenric. A split second later, Hnagi was hurled through the air.

Kenric caught Mordig's stones with one hand. His father called out to him. "Here!"

Kenric dropped the amulet into his pocket and turned. Brogan knelt and shoved the sword toward him. It skimmed along the paving stones, and Kenric reached down to grab it.

He misjudged how fast it was coming. The razor-sharp edge sliced at his fingers. Blood welled up in the cut and dripped onto the blade.

A pale blue-white flame sprang to life along the blade. *Blood is to bind it,* Kenric remembered.

The magic flared up the sword until it reached Kenric's hand, making it tingle. The sensation crept up his arm, straight through to his heart. His heart seemed to grow fuller and fuller until he was sure it would swell out of his chest.

He looked up from the blade and saw Mordig striding toward him, sword drawn. Linwe darted forward, trying to give Kenric some time. She held her sword high to parry the warlord's blow.

Mordig's sword crashed down on her. She stumbled backward, struggling to keep her footing. Before she had regained her balance, Mordig rushed her, sword raised.

The blow would kill her, Kenric was certain. King Thorgil's words rang in his head. *Strike first in love, so evil can't find it.*

Kenric threw himself forward, blade outstretched. He struck Linwe across the back of her legs with the flat of the blade. She fell face-first in the dirt.

Mordig shifted his course and charged straight for Kenric.

Kenric knelt in the dirt and braced himself. He gathered his strength to hold his ground. He held the blade of power high and gritted his teeth.

Mordig swung his sword. Stunned, Kenric watched the glowing power of his blade repel Mordig's blow. The warlord's head jerked back in surprise. Before he could check his stride, his momentum carried him forward. He ran straight into the blade of power, impaling himself on the glowing sword.

Mordig cried out in anguish. The sound made Kenric's blood curdle, but still he held firm.

Mordig's face was inches from Kenric's. Through the narrow slits in his helm, Kenric could see the warlord's eyes widen in shock and pain. The light of the sword grew brighter and brighter. It was as if it had somehow caught fire inside Mordig's body. The white light filled Mordig until he began to glow like a burning ember. Kenric watched in horror. Mordig's body, nothing but a burned shell, crumbled in on itself.

Kenric felt a gentle brush against his shoulder. He looked around, but there was nothing there. *See? A small flame can bring down a house. Nicely done, young smith.* King Thorgil's voice whispered in his ear. Kenric saw his faded wraithlike form swirl by. Then it disappeared into the first gray light of morning.

He was gone, Kenric realized. King Thorgil had died with Mordig. They had defeated the warlord, but lost their king.

Kenric let go of the blade and stumbled away.

Mordig's army still stood in front of them, stretched out as far as the eye could see. Linwe picked herself up off the ground. Limping, she came to stand next to him. Her arm hung strangely at her side, as if she had injured it. "Sometime soon, you will tell me why you struck me down."

"You don't know?" he asked, surprised.

Her eyes narrowed as she thought. "The prophecy? The one Artemus and Thulidor were explaining to you?"

Kenric nodded. "I had to strike first in, er, love." Cheeks flaming, he rushed to add, "To season the blade." Anxious to change the subject, he looked back to Mordig's army. "Now what do we do?" he asked.

"Now we no longer fight alone," Linwe said. She pointed to the east.

Kenric saw two bulky figures leading an entire army of goblin warriors. Prince Durrig and King Orlegg! They'd come in time!

A horn sounded to the west, and Kenric turned. The rising sun glinted off the armor of a second army. At the front rode a tall, slender figure in silver mail. Her long black hair rippled in the breeze. Princess Tamaril! The armies of Fey and man had made it as well.

Exhaustion began to swamp him. Kenric shook his head, trying to clear it.

He felt a hand on his shoulder, and then he was caught in a giant bear hug. "Well done, son. Well done," his father said.

Another trumpet sounded. Kenric looked up. Three Sleäg stepped forward from the ranks of Mordig's army. They held a white banner.

Princess Tamaril rode forward on her horse. King Orlegg walked on one side, Prince Durrig on the other. They halted when they reached Kenric's small group. "My father was right," the princess said. "You were our hope in this darkness. Thank you."

Then she turned to Linwe and held out her hand. "Come, Princess. The rulers of Lowthar have a surrender to see to."

Linwe stared at the hand for a moment. Then, using her good hand, she reached out and clasped it. Tamaril pulled her onto the back of the horse. She gave Linwe a moment to settle herself. Then she snapped the reins and rode toward the Sleäg.

The horse pranced around a small, still shape.

"Hnagi!" Kenric started to run to the goblin's side, but his father pulled him back.

Hnagi lifted his head. "Is over?" he asked.

"Yes," Brogan called out. "The fighting is over."

The little goblin struggled to his feet. He swayed slightly as he began to walk toward Kenric. He stumbled, and was quickly surrounded by finnboggi. They clustered around him and lifted him onto their shoulders.

The finnboggi carried Hnagi and gently set him down in front of Kenric. The little goblin had a cut on his cheek, and one of his ears was bent funny. One by one, the finnboggi lifted their hands to their hearts. Hnagi did the same.

Slowly, Kenric lifted his hand to his own heart, and smiled.

"Now," Hnagi said. "Now can Hnagi have firestone back?"

❧ 19 ❧

Two weeks later, a crowd stood gathered around the ward stone. Kenric saw Linwe, with her arm in a sling, standing next to Cerinor. Beside them were Thulidor and Rindelorn. Even King Valorin had come, although he still looked weak from Mordig's influence. Kenric spotted Kraag and Prince Durrig in the large group of goblins.

As Kenric stood between his father and mother, the light breeze ruffled his hair. The sky was a piercing blue with fluffy white clouds. It was hard to believe that evil had come so close to destroying it all.

"Come forward, Kenric of Penrith," Princess Tamaril called out. As all eyes turned toward him he fought the urge to shrink back against his father. Shyly, he stepped before the princess.

"You have shown great honor and courage, young smith. Your love for your father gave you the strength to look evil in the face and call it such. Your love for your king"—Tamaril's voice faltered the tiniest bit—"gave you the heart to rally the races of Lowthar to his cause. And your love for our land gave you the courage to conquer that evil once and for all."

She put her hand out to Artemus, who placed something in it. The princess held up the object. It was a bloodstone hanging from a silver chain. She slipped the chain over Kenric's head. "You have proven yourself as worthy as any knight of our realm. Let this bloodstone bind to you as you have bound your loyalty to our land. You have our utmost thanks."

Kenric now had a bound stone! Just like a knight. He felt his cheeks grow hot. He fought the urge to grab the bloodstone and take a closer look.

As he stepped back to stand beside his father, Cerinor spoke. "We have come through a great trial together," the Fey elder said. "It is only because the three races stood together that we are here today. It is time for a new beginning. What better place than in the spot where it all began?

"The old ways must make way for the new. The days of kings are over. Lowthar shall be ruled by a council of three times three. From each race, three protectors shall work with the others to keep our land safe. From each race, there shall be one of royal blood." Linwe and Prince Durrig stepped forward into the circle to stand with Princess Tamaril.

"And from each race, someone to remember the old lore," Cerinor's voice continued.

Skogul, the goblin bard, took off his brooch and presented it to Hnagi. Hnagi looked back at him, confused. Then the old bard gently shoved the little goblin forward. Stunned, Hnagi took his place next to Rindelorn and Artemus. All the finnboggi cheered.

"And lastly, from each race, a smith. So we will always have the means to forge a new blade of power, should the need arise," Cerinor said.

Thulidor and Kraag stepped forward into the circle. There was a pause while everyone waited for the human smith to come forward. Finally Kenric's father gave him a gentle nudge.

Kenric's eyes widened in shock. He gave the princess a questioning look. She nodded her head. "My father knew he would not survive Mordig's death. His last wish was that you should be rightfully honored by the races of Lowthar."

In wonder, Kenric stepped forward. As he took his place in the circle, the crowd around the ward stone cheered.

"Well done, young smith," Princess Tamaril said.